Satellites Gone

By: Tim Attewell

I wrote all of these for Angel Bellmer, who picked me up, straightened me out, and turned my life around.

Thank you. I love you.

Thank you for reading *Satellites Gone*
If you end up enjoying these stories, please take a moment to leave
a quick comment or review on Amazon. Maybe leave some stars,
while you're at it.

Your response to this book will be infinitely helpful and deeply
appreciated.

OUTROS

Music played a major role in pushing me towards making a career in storytelling. In high school, I was absolutely devastated to hear that I couldn't freely use the beautiful work of James Horner, Hans Zimmer, Alan Silvestri, etc. because of something called "copyright law." My heart started to sing last year when I realized that my love of music could once again be joined with my stories.

Each one of these shorts has a song pinned to its ending. They're at the end for a reason. I don't want my skewed taste in music to alter your reading experience before you even start. When you're done, and the imaginary credits start to roll, I'd like a shot at striking a chord with you. Wish me luck.

If you're interested in pursuing this extra credit and listening between reads, I've made it easy for you. Simply search Spotify or Youtube for a playlist entitled "Satellites Gone." There, you will find the wonderful soundtrack to this book. I hope you enjoy it.

CONTENTS

JOHNNY

Judging by the fidelity of Maggie's voice, she was calling from her cell phone instead of her office; technically not allowed, but no one was keeping track.

"This one's a rush," she said.

"Aren't they all?" I rolled up to my desk, ready to type. "Go ahead."

She gave me everything I needed, name, phone number, I.P. address, timeframe.

"I really mean rush," she added. "I've got a meeting coming up."

"Alright. Priorities?"

"Phone transcripts. E-mails of note," she said. "I need a complete timeline."

"So my priorities are… everything?"

I could tell she was in a genuine rush. Normally she keeps me on the line just as a distraction from work, chatting about this and that, procrastination under the guise of business. Instead she simply said, "Catch up later," and ended the call.

I unwrapped my turkey sandwich, took a bite, and started blasting my way through the encryptions that protected the case's privacy.

His name was Tom Lee, and he was dead. The security of his wireless service provider opened like a zipper. The first call I transcribed was between Tom Lee and a woman named Valerie. In the file I was composing, I labeled his voice as "nervous vibrato." Sometimes I got in trouble for being eccentric in my descriptions, but I lacked other emotional outlets so the labels remained. No one fired me.

He called her on September 20th, four and a half rings before she picked up. I started typing.

Valerie: TTooooommmmmm!
I liked to include as much expression as possible.
Tom: Hey, are you, uh. Are you busy right now?
Valerie: I'm about to run out the door but I have a few minutes. Are you still sick?
Tom: I don't... I don't know. Not like I was before, but...
Valerie: It got worse? It's not the flu is it?
Tom: No, nothing like that. That was just a cold and it's gone, but now something else is happening. I'm sorry. I don't want to worry you.
Valerie: Tom, what is it?
Tom: I don't know how to say this. Jesus, I don't want to sound crazy. I've been feeling like... like I'm not alone, I guess? But I should be. You know how in some movies people say they feel like they're being watched and you think, "What could that possibly feel like?"
Valerie: Yeah.
Tom: I feel like that all the time now.
Valerie: Like you're being watched?
Tom: Maybe studied? [Nervous laughter] It sounds ridiculous now that I said it out loud.
Valerie: How long has this been going on?

Tom: Ever since I got over the cold, a couple days. My—my appetite is gone and I'm having trouble sleeping, and... I don't know.

Valerie: It sounds like stress, like a lot. Is everything okay at work?

Tom: Probably. I haven't gone in since I started coughing.

Valerie: Okay. Have you been leaving the house at all?

Tom: I haven't been in the mood. I guess maybe that's the problem, isn't it?

Valerie: Maybe?

Tom: So what should I—

Valerie: You should—sorry, go ahead.

Tom: No, you go.

Valerie: I was just going to say you should go outside. Put your shoes on and go for a walk. Right now. Friend's orders.

Tom: Right. Right. Clear my head. Fresh air and all that.

Valerie: It never fails. [Car door opens, shuts] But if it does, let me know. Okay?

Tom: Sure. It sounds like you've got to go.

Valerie: I can talk and drive. It's not that hard.

Tom: No, I know you're busy. How's things with you? Fam ok?

Valerie: Everything's pretty good. Jes has been acting up in school. She used her first curse word. I'm going in to talk to her teacher now.

Tom: That's good, that's good.

Valerie: You're pretty distracted right now, aren't you?

Tom: What?

Valerie: Go take a walk, Tom. And call me any time. If this gets better or worse I want to hear about it.

Tom: What if it stays the same?

Valerie: [sigh] Call no matter what.

Tom: Sounds good.

Valerie: Are you sure you don't want to talk more right now? It's a ten minute drive and I'm just going to get depressed listening to talk radio.

Tom: Probably less depressing than talking to your crazy friend.

Valerie: You're not crazy. Do you have anyone you can hang out with over there?

Tom: No, I... you know. I think it's hard to make new friends when you move. But I was thinking maybe it's time to start planning a trip out to you? I'm not inviting myself, just an idea.

Valerie: That would be great. We'll have a bed made and waiting for you.

Tom: Great.

Valerie: Ok. Talk soon? I want updates.

Tom: Sure.

[...]

Valerie: Alright. Enjoy your walk.

Tom: Will do. Thanks for talking.

Valerie: Any time.

Tom: Wait, Valerie?

Valerie: Yeah?

Tom: Was there someone named Johnny in our high school?

Valerie: Johnny... I don't think so.

Tom: Ok, thanks again.

Valerie: Wait, why?

Tom: I just keep feeling like I know someone named Johnny.

Valerie: That's a pretty strange thing to say, Tom.

Tom: Yup. I'll let you go.

Valerie: [Laughs] Ok. Take care.

I took a break to stretch my fingers and do some reading. Carpal tunnel can be devastating for someone in my line of work. After I got the job, the very same guy that swore me to an agreement of non-disclosure at penalty of death was kind enough to show me a few exercises to keep my hands healthy.

Three sets of ten finger extension exercises later, I got hold of Tom's obituary. It would go later in the timeline but I liked to break up my transcribing with some search, copy, and paste. The obit was as nicely written as it was inaccurate.

"Tom Lee, age 38, passed away in his Brooklyn apartment on September 25th, 2018. He was born in Long Beach, CA, and frequently wrote poems in his free time, some of which were published. He had moved to New York for work just one month prior to his passing. Tom is survived by no immediate family, but his friends from home say they will always remember him."

When obits describe the cause of death, there's a pretty limited array of descriptions they give. It can be "passed peacefully," or "passed suddenly." Stuff like that. If they say "suddenly," it's usually followed up with a cause, like heart attack or accident. Otherwise, things are kept politely vague. Without "peacefully" or "suddenly," it can mean anything, usually not a good way to go. I hated how bland the stories had to be. I understood why it was that way, especially for a case like this, but understanding and liking are two different things.

No one, other than essential personnel, would ever know Tom's true story.

His next significant contact was with Valerie again. He e-mailed her the next morning.

From: Tom
To: Valerie
Subject: Johnny

Hey, thanks for talking yesterday. I woke up feeling a little better. Had some crazy dreams but it feels like they squeezed all the crazy out of me.

Thanks again,

-Tom

Valerie texted Tom back thirty minutes later.

Valerie: *Glad you're feeling better. What are your plans for the day?*

Tom: *I don't know yet. I got invited to a co-worker's birthday.*

Valerie: *Sounds like fun.*

Tom: *You don't know the co-worker. I should probably go, shouldn't I?*

Valerie: *Please go.*

Tom: *I might still be contagious?*

Valerie: *[link to WebMD.com regarding common cold]*

Valerie: *[Smiley Emoji]*

Two hours passed before Valerie texted again.

Valerie: *So what's the plan? Still feeling good?*

Tom: *I think I'm gonna go!*

I took another break when I realized I forgot to eat my sandwich. Eating is the ultimate excuse to take a break from typing, hacking, etc. Surviving my work was kind of a mental dance. It took pretending I was in a normal office, working a normal job. Sometimes I actually said, "just another day at the office" out loud, just to stay straight. I browsed the news, but all of it had turned into weather. Wildfires in the West, Hurricane Cynthia in the East. If only those two could meet.

An e-mail came through from Sarah in booking. She had a knack for drawing and liked to do sketches of the entities that got locked up during her shift. I agreed to join her mailing list because I never got to see the things, but stopped opening the attachments about a week later. The entities were rarely benevolent-looking.

I finished eating and got back to work. A couple hours after texting with Valerie, Tom sent a message to a woman name Kim. I confirmed my obvious assumption with a quick Google search, no hacking necessary. Kim was Tom's co-worker. Tom texted:

Tom: *Heading over!*

His message received no reply, and later that night he called Valerie, who answered in two rings.

Valerie: *Hi Tom.*
Tom: *Hey. I'm not calling to late am I?*
Valerie: *It's only nine here. You're fine.*
[...]
Valerie: *Did you go to that thing?*
Tom: *Just for a little. I felt... uh, well... it was a weird party. Everyone—*
Valerie: *Weird?*
Tom: *...had knives in their pockets.*
Valerie: *Everyone had what?*
Tom: *Knives. Some were butter knives but most were like, steak knives or pocket knives. Some people were actually wearing them around their belts, like Rambo or something.*
Valerie: *Jesus, who is this birthday guy?*
Tom: *She. And I don't know, just someone at work. She had a knife too.*

Valerie: I'm so confused. What were they doing with their knives? Was it like a themed party or something?

Tom: No, it was just a regular party. They all just had knives and some of them were serrated and I was the only one who didn't have one and—

Valerie: So they were just waving them around or something?

Tom: No, I couldn't actually see them.

[...]

Valerie: So how did you know they had knives?

Tom: [Laughter] I don't... know? I was sure...

Valerie: Tom.

Tom: It was like how in dreams you just know something is true. Well, I knew they had knives.

Valerie: I'm going to say something and I don't want you to take offense. I'm your friend and I just want the best for you.

Tom: You think I should go to the hospital.

Valerie: Yeah.

Tom: Maybe I will tomorrow. Maybe I just need sleep.

Valerie: Wouldn't it be better to talk to a doctor? Be around people?

Tom: Valerie. I'm not going to hurt myself if that's what you're thinking. I promise. I'm kind of freaking out, but I'm not in that kind of freak out. I promise I'll go to the hospital if it gets worse.

Valerie: Ok. Do you want to talk until you get tired?

Tom: No, that's ok. I'm sorry I bothered you. Sometimes it helps to just hear yourself say this stuff out loud, you know?

Valerie: You mentioned that before, and you're never bothering me, Tom. You never did.

[...]

Tom: Thanks.

Valerie: I mean that. In every way.

Tom: Same. It would really be nice to visit again.

Valerie: Book a flight.
Tom: I'll do that.
Valerie: Okay, I better—
Tom: Yeah, me too. Sleep and all that.
Valerie: Ok. Good night, Tom.
Tom: Goodnight.

Tom did not buy a plane ticket that night. I think he had a really rough time, but that's just conjecture. He had no contact with the outside world until 9AM the next day. He called three different numbers, all cognitive behavioral therapists. All went to voicemail. Standard, since they spend all day with patients. The first therapist was named Lindsay McMann.

Lindsay's Voicemail: Hi, you've reached Lindsay McMann. If you are in crisis, please hang up and dial 9-1-1. Otherwise, please leave a message with your name, number, and a brief description of why you're calling. I will get back to you during the next business day at the absolute latest. Thank you.
Tom: Hey. My name is Tom, and... well I'm not sure how to describe this. There was this thing where I thought people had knives on them and now I don't trust what I'm seeing but I also don't want to leave my apartment. Um…
[…]
Tom's pause was long enough to activate the auto response:
Voicemail System: If you are finished recording, press one. If you would like to—
Tom ended the call.

He had two more nearly identical interactions with psychologist voicemails. Immediately after that he made a slew of Google searches, all dancing around the same subject:

"long black bugs"

"finger sized black bugs"
"new species of roach in new york"
"insect black big six legs pinchers"
"roach black big six legs fangs"
"breaking news people seeing strange bug new york"
"bug infestation breaking news"
"invasive insects poisonous"
"what are the new bugs in new york?"
"Are there new insects in new york?"
"Seeing bugs mental illness"
"Imaginary bugs"
"Insect hallucination"
"Ekbom's syndrome"
"Ekbom's syndrome treatment"

The syndrome he found was just a scientific name for his self-diagnosis. The guy was seeing bugs that weren't there. I got up for a stretch and went for a stroll around the office, just another day. My co-workers gave polite smiles and one-beat waves, but made no conversation. People on my floor aren't exactly the social type.

I needed the social type, though. To fill the void, I headed down to the commissary and bought a Powerade, just because I knew the lady at the cash register would be willing to chat. She must have called in sick, because there was a guy I didn't recognize standing in her place. I bought the Powerade anyway and headed back to my floor. On the elevator ride up, I got my fix.

"Did you hear?" a man from admin asked. I couldn't remember his name.

"About what?"

"A 2-1-9 broke loose in the East Europe Branch."

"Yeesh," I said, then realized I might have just become a liability. "Wait, am I allowed to know about that?"

"No secret, no worries. We're sending out a security memo in a few minutes."

My floor came first. I got out and asked, "How bad is it?"

"Bad."

The doors closed. Back to work.

Tom was all silent on the cyber front until the night that followed his bug Google-spree. No human contact, but he took down a note on his phone. It was backed up to his cloud server at 2AM.

Venting. Therapists didn't call back yet and I don't want to worry Valerie. Talked myself out of the bugs since they're not real. Went for a walk which was a mistake. It was like I was being followed. I could almost hear footsteps. Who is Johnny? Do I know a Johnny? Is it possible to get a name stuck in your head? I constantly have this feeling like I want to turn around and say something to him. Speaking of things being stuck in my head. This:

You can't get untangled
From your sweet and bloody sheets
Under, over, lost inside them
What a place to die

What song is that? It's been stuck in my head since my walk. Something is really really wrong I don't know what to do. Can you help me, notepad? Just tried to get into bed but couldn't. Something about that song told me not to. Probably the thing about bloody sheets and dying hahahaha. Going to sleep on rug without sheets. Use coats to stay comfy. Someday I'll read this and cringe and delete it and be glad I got over it.

Valerie called the next day. Tom didn't answer. She left this voicemail.

Valerie: Heeeyyyy. Just checking in. I hope things are getting brighter. They better be, because if they're not and you haven't called me to talk, then our friendship is over. Oh, and I told Jes you might be visiting and she called you "Uncle Tom." I had to explain that not all of mommy's guy friends are brothers. So then she asked if you were my boyfriend... So. Yeah. Ok, I gotta go but please call me. Byyyee.

Tom texted back an hour later.

Tom: Hey! Sorry, been playing catch up at work. Crazy couple days. Will call u back when I get a sec.
Valerie: Good! Book a flight yet?

Tom gave no answer. All three therapists returned Tom's calls and started by saying he should go to a hospital. Two were booked solid. One didn't have an opening until five days later. Tom would be dead in two. His next Google spree spelled it out.

"man made of grey tar"
"man with bones sticking out from skin"
"dripping man"
"grey man in hoodie Johnny"
"man in hoodie hallucination"
"creature in hoodie hallucination"
"creature dark grey viscous skin"
"grey fluid skin man named Johnny"
"man with eight limbs grey"
"grey goo skin song lyrics"
"Sweet bloody sheets song lyrics"
"grey goo hoodie peripheral vision"
"things you can only see in your peripheral vision"
"grey figure peripheral vision not ghost"

"What do I do if I see someone in the corner of my eye?"
"Man johnny can't look directly at"
"safe to close eyes if evil presence in peripheral vision?"

Sage from accounting interrupted my work to tell me there were brownies in the rec room.

"Awesome," I said. "Thanks." We shared a fist bump and I went straight back to work.

Tom ignored all incoming calls, texts, and e-mails for the next twenty-four hours. The next item in the timeline was another notepad doc, uploaded to the cloud.

I know who's been doing it. His name is Johnny and I never met him. I don't know if he wants to hurt me but I do know that he hates me. His words kind of gurgle out of his mouth. I don't even think it's a mouth. I don't think it moves. I pretended to sleep earlier and could hear him get close. Gurgling over me. He dripped that stuff on me but when I opened my eyes he was gone and so was the stuff. He's watching me from the corner of the room but only when I'm looking away. I would run away but he's made the bugs rise. He's made them over three feet deep outside. I can see them down there. They're like a swamp that moves.

Valerie called and left a voicemail the next day.

Valerie: *Hey, I was worried so I tried you at work and they said you haven't been in all week. If you don't call me back in ten minutes I'm going to buy a flight just to come check on you. I mean it. Call me back. I'm worried.*

She followed through, and booked flight DL 4589, LGB to JFK for that evening. Later, right around the time she boarding, Tom was on the phone with a 9-1-1 operator.

Operator: 9-1-1 what's your emergency?
Tom: I'm having a crisis.
Operator: What is your crisis, sir? Are you in danger?
Tom: I think so. Johnny keeps getting closer and I *[hysterical laughter] AND I DON'T THINK HE WANTS A HUG. [more laughter.]*
Operator: What's your location?
Tom: 283 Sixth Avenue. Brooklyn.
Operator: And is Johnny threatening you?
Tom: [Laughter]
Operator: Sir, are you able to get to safety?
Tom: [Intermittent laughter] I can't get away from my eyes! There is a sea of bugs up to my third story window and the glass is cracking. Everything is so sharp. So sharp.
Operator: Is there someplace safe you can get to? A closet or a neighbor? Police are on their way.

Tom's next and last words were said with incredible calm. There were a lot of non-verbal sounds that followed, something like the crackling of a fire, gurgling, and laughter with every "hah" a deliberate, perfectly enunciated clone of the last, like panting, only with vowels. It's difficult to tell whether or not the laughter was Tom's.

Prior to that three-minute stretch of horrible sounds, though, Tom's final words were uttered with casual serenity. Right around the time that Valerie's plane had pushed back from the departure gate, and when the police were about eight blocks away, Tom let out a tired, reluctant sigh, and said:

Tom: He's breaking. My fingers.

The police report, which was immediately confiscated by the F.B.I., which was swiftly kicked over to us at G.T.I., gave a fairly detailed summary. Tom was dead on arrival. The crackling sound of the fire had in fact been every single one of Tom's finger and toe joints snapping. His body was found sitting upright in the corner of his living room in a "meditative stance" with a viscous grey substance dripping from all of his facial orifices. The coroner later determined that the Tom's eyes, ears, nostrils, and mouth had been used as inlets to pump in an "excessive amount" of the grey substance. The substance completely filled the victim's lungs and stomach, which was ruptured by the pressure.

The night after the autopsy, a security system was triggered in the morgue. Although motion was detected, nothing showed up on the CCTV cameras. The coroner later reported to the FBI that the grey substance had completely "vacated" the body and could not be found anywhere on the premises.

That just about concluded my timeline and report. I submitted my findings to Maggie and got a call back about ten minutes later.

"Hey Maggie."

"Hey Vince. Got the e-mail. I'm about to step into a meeting. Could you sum it up?"

"They don't pay me to theorize," I said. "I'm just the guy with the keyboard."

"Don't be a dick."

"Sorry. Based on the guy's description it was definitely 5-3-1 again."

"Which one is that?" Maggie asked. I could hear her heels clopping on the floor of whatever hallway she was in.

"Johnny."

"Right," she said. "Ok, anything new that I can pass along to the boss?"

"Not really," I replied. "The song lyrics were a little more coherent."

"But still scaring the guy away from his bed? Keeping him from sleeping?"

"Yup."

"And the goo got away?"

"Yup."

"I hate this thing," Maggie said. "Did we at least get some clues on why it calls itself Johnny?"

"Maggie. If I had any news I would give it to you."

She sighed. "I know. I've just been getting hassled for progress."

"Like that's in your control."

"I keep saying 'Talk to the field guys,' but he doesn't want to hear it." She groaned. "Did you still want to get dinner tonight?"

"Not sure I'll want to eat," I said. "The 9-1-1 wasn't really hunger-inducing."

"I get it. What about yoga tomorrow morning?"

"Game on," I said.

"Awesome. Talk soon."

"Yah."

The rest of my day was pretty mellow. I didn't have any complete profiles or timelines to build, just a collection of random, unrelated phone and e-mail hacks. I didn't have the inside scoop from Maggie on those, so I had no idea what I was transcribing. All I had to go on was the steadfast rule: The more mundane a conversation is, the more significant it is. Its participants just have better code words.

I had enough years under my belt that if I decided to duck out a half hour early, no one would really care. So that's what I did. On my way out, I took a moment to stop in the lobby and appreciate that they were finally done renovating. The new frosted windows and artificial daylight outside were really convincing. If not for my commute, I would forget how far below the surface I was working.

Security was as thorough as ever: full body scan, x-ray, and pockets. They checked the implant in my neck to make sure it would explode if I said anything about my job to a non-employee.

I only had to wait a few minutes for the next employee tram to arrive. I got on, and as it glided through the cave network, I struggled against the urge to imagine Johnny's face. Best to leave work at work and numbered entities to themselves.

I smiled and nodded at every employee that stepped onto the tram, doing my part to make sure that the job was a pleasant one. My stop came, and I was the only one to get off. There are some days that I'm happy to have the elevator all to myself. This was not one of them. Even a silent stranger would have made the ride to the surface more pleasant.

I reached the surface and stepped out, into the back room of one of the many Dollar Stores G.T.I. used to hide its service elevators in plain sight. After whistling my way across the parking lot to my car, I took a ten-minute detour to my semi-usual stop at "Craig's Trophy and Engraving." Craig was a good guy; we were on a first name basis. He always had my custom design and template ready to go. Since I was a regular, he always took care of my engravings the moment I ordered them. Craig had also learned not to ask questions, even though there was no way he believed my cover story of the plaques being "movie props."

After buying the custom plaque, I headed home and threw food in the microwave. It was unlikely that I would actually manage to eat any of it, but worth a shot. While the food cooked, I found a flattering photo of Tom Lee, printed it out, and cut it down to a three-by-three inch square.

My custom plaque was pretty simple, more like the base of a trophy without a tower sticking out of it. Instead, its top surface had a slim, three-inch slot to hold a photo upright and a circle for a candle, deep enough so only the flame was showing.

I placed the stand on the table, opposite me, and lit the candle just in time for the microwave to beep. Dinner time. I sat across from Tom with my food and appreciated the custom engraving on the stand, the truth he deserved that his obituary was forbidden to say.

Tom Lee
Died in agony from an encounter with Entity Five Three One.
Your story is remembered.

There was always an off-chance that a stray 0-1-2 whisked his consciousness away to a better place, but word around the office was that those were a dying breed.

I managed to eat half of my dinner before I pushed it aside, opting to sit in silence and watch the memorial flame dance itself into darkness.

"Hand Covers Bruise" – Trent Reznor, Atticus Ross

WASTED GATES

DAY 643

Well, I guess I'll admit for the record that today's opening of The Gates of Hell was a complete disaster. The lair was perfect. Security was tight. I had everything I needed. What went wrong I never could have anticipated. Criminy, give me some young adventurer with a hat and a hero complex and let him stop me; anything is better than this.

I've been trying to figure out how to move on, but I don't even want to get out of bed. I have so many workers to layoff… was really counting on a biblical apocalypse to terminate their employment for me. I'll leave the gate as is, I guess, maybe move it to storage and save some money.

I can't help but feel time creeping up on me. Having been after this dream for so long, how much longer could I possibly have to make my mark on the world? Sure, I could melt a monument or maybe try a man-made earthquake, but who respects the guy who takes the easy target?

Every now and then I think I better just cut my losses and retire to some fishing hole. The fantasy never lasts longer than twenty seconds.

Dead tired and need to sleep now. Tomorrow I'll start firing people early and hopefully be done by lunch.

DAY 645

The layoffs weren't as bad as I thought. We were able to launch the majority of our employees into orbit and I expect they will be out of breathable air within a couple days. The few that remain have become extremely loyal.

Was feeling a lot better about things until we found out the gate can't be moved. Scorch, my right hand man, tells me that by opening the portal, the materials that form the gate have accrued an absurd amount of dark matter. It's about as heavy as the Sears Tower now.

With that, my dreams of renting out the lair for special events have been dashed. Being in close proximity to the gate renders feelings of dissatisfaction, thus turning away any potential tenants. Some millionaire brought his daughter in to explore the possibility of hosting her birthday party in the space. Within twenty minutes, they were questioning the very idea of celebrating, since birthdays are really just another milestone in the slow march towards death.

I'm trying to maintain a positive attitude. Over the next few days we'll try and make the whole dark matter issue work in our favor. I'll have to get my hands dirty due to lack of manpower, but we'll be digging out a space deep under the gate. When we're ready, we'll blow out the floor and drop it far enough that the lair isn't within its area of influence. With the gate out of sight the lair will be much easier to lease.

None of this would be a problem, of course, if the underworld had been what I thought it would be. I had envisioned an explosive blast of evil and pain that would consume this worthless planet in one sweep. Instead, I was confronted with complete and utter apathy. The portal is wide open, but it seems that the dark realm is completely disinterested in our world. People we send either don't come back, or return with no memory of what they saw, not a drop of blood on them.

I haven't a clue how to close the gate so... open it shall remain. Rather than riding a wave of outpouring agony and death, I'll be sitting in bars, showing people pictures of the gate on my phone. Even photos won't bring me notoriety. I snapped off quite a few before I realized there was no way to do it justice. The obsidian texture doesn't come through, and the whole thing looks two-thirds its actual size.

It really is gorgeous, I'm telling you. The rusted iron frame holds its perfect circle of custom-formed beautiful black obsidian in place. Activating the portal did not yield the swirling and/or fleshy vortex I anticipated, but rather, a perfect red velvet curtain appeared in a blink. It was a very theatrical look for an interdimensional portal. I didn't mind it, but when nothing emerged from said curtains, my heart sank.

Scorch encourages me to write about my feelings rather than take them out on people. It feels good to let out my despair.

Have to go now. Our digging is taking us pretty close to the gate and if we don't quickly rotate diggers, the shoveling stops due to gate-induced-depression. We're trying to get the space clear and rentable in time for wedding season.

DAY 651

Things have been so completely insane the last couple of days that I haven't had a second to write. Lots to catch up on. We successfully dropped the gate about fifty feet below the rest of the lair. In doing so it fell completely flat and, seeing as how it is impossible to lift, I suppose it will remain that way for quite some time. Oddly enough, its new position seems to have had no effect on the hanging red velvet curtain, making it more of a carpet than drape.

Once I beheld this sight, a solution came to me. If the forces of the underworld are completely disinterested in the inhabitants of ours, perhaps we can coax them out by taking a page out of the book of fishing. Scorch and I have spent recent days traveling the globe in search of various high value religious icons and tokens, both good and evil. It is my masterful plan to, over the coming days, dangle these items down through the curtain into hell in the hopes of getting a bite.

This will, of course, be a matter of trial and error, as I am uncertain how easy it will be to pull out anything that grabs hold on the other end. My understanding of what lies on the other side of those velvet waves is cursory at best. Every employee I've sent through the portal has lost contact and failed to return. I had tried attaching tethers to some of them, but once we pulled them back, they would retain no memory of what they had seen or done on the other side, even if they had been there for days.

In hindsight, I definitely should have sent the layoffs through the curtain rather than rocketing them into airless outer space, but I was tired at the time and perhaps not making logical decisions.

We tried sending a camera through as well, but it only sent back a repeating signal of some kind of game show that completely lacked contestants. The show's host, a man devoid of body language who never smiled, would ask trivia questions to a line-up of five empty podiums. I've been meaning to go back and analyze the footage, but honestly, it's so dreadfully boring that I always find myself falling asleep. Maybe that's the whole point.

Scorch has been doing great work. After the religious iconography heists, he willingly took on the role of property manager for the lair. He's a man that's willing to do what is necessary for the cause, even if it means working two jobs without a pay raise. In watching him work from my control room, I've found that he has quite a knack for hosting open houses. It turns out he's got a lot of charisma stuffed up his sleeve, and people seem to hardly notice the grotesque burns across his face and chest.

Very eager to try out our fishing technique so I'll have to keep this short. Will report back with updates.

DAY 660

As I write, the god awful bass pulse of a DJ's ego thumps in my ears. A terrible nuisance, but well worth it for the money. So far we've had no wedding bookings, but the rave scene seems utterly entranced with the space. Scorch and I duck in every thirty minutes, like parents checking on kids engrossed in a slumber party. We watch the dancing, convulsing, half-nude drug users do their thing as long as we can stomach. We never stay long as the music is loud and the people are intolerable. I can't help but smirk at how little they know about what immense power yawns beneath their feet.

I'm writing now sitting on the ledge of our velvet pond to hell. My fishing line has swayed and twitched, but sadly I have yet to get anything to grab hold long enough for me to pull.

Really starting to question what all of this is for. So what if I end this world? There will always be another. In a universe so vast, how can anyone make a truly meaningful impact? Starting to suspect Scorch is losing faith in me. It hurts to see him turn so suddenly.

Ah, stupid me. I've been sitting here for well over fifteen minutes. Disregard that last paragraph, I need to go back topside and clear my head of the Gate's despairing vibes.

It really is a tough spot to be in this weekend. One form of hell below us and another above. Hope we can get new tenants soon. How long can people possibly dance for, anyway?

DAY 664

Still no firm bites, only nibbles and gentle tugs. Relieved at least to see our electronic dance tenants clear out. I kept their security deposit. We'll have some peace and quiet around here until next week. Some kind of card game tournament is moving in. Not clear on the rules of *Magic: the Gathering* but it can't be any worse than the last group.

Did something I shouldn't have yesterday. Such is the result of desperation, I guess. Tied off a rope and took a dip beyond the velvet curtain. Scorch didn't want to do it, but he knew if he didn't help I would probably never return.

All is well that ends well, though. Scorch pulled me back to the surface and, as feared, I had no recollection of my time below. He said my eyes looked wet but, smart man, he explained it away as an allergic reaction.

It just now occurred to me that although we've tried human memory and digital recording, there has been no effort to document the under-happenings with old fashioned pen and paper. If I secure a separate line to this very journal, I will—

You know what? No time to explain. I must wake Scorch right away. Who knows what I might record? Perhaps scholars will analyze my next passage for decades to come. Maybe I have found my true calling: to be the first eye-witness of what lies below. My next entry shall be from the dark realm. Wish me luck.

DAY NEVER

I'm a virgin.

Unless blow up dolls count.
I wet the bed two years ago.
I wasn't the bully. I starved every day.
I never fought a CIA agent.
I do not communicate with alien intelligences.
I'm just lonely and I want to punish the world for it.
I'm in love with Scorch but don't know how to tell him.

DAY 665

Amazing discovery! The underworld possesses a potent deceiving power! If you analyze the handwriting there is no way of distinguishing the lies of the dark realm from my own script. The things written above, though quite a stretch, were clearly devised to bring me pure suffering and sorrow here in the real world. Devious, indeed. Imagine the potential if this force could be released on the entire world! More on this later; can't wait for my next trip to Hell!

DAY 666

Uneventful. No progress.

DAY 667

I'm a nobody. I'll always be a nobody. When I went down there, Scorch brought my journal up first. He says he didn't read it but I'm pretty sure he did. He's been acting really weird around me. This is so uncomfortable. I want to die.

The *Magic: the Gathering* card game tournament is moving in. I was really hoping it would be something cooler, but they don't even gamble.

DAY 676

Sorry it's been so long. I've been too miserable to write. Finally got a mood boost from the clown convention we hosted at the lair today. I'll admit I wasn't high on the idea at first, but Scorch convinced me that money is money. Once they arrived, the idea struck me. Devious, exciting, and just what I needed to jump out of this awful depression.

It was brilliantly easy. They're clowns. They love theatrics. So when I marched them single file down to the gate and told them that the 'surprise party room' was on the other side, they all leapt for it. The head clown was even delighted to have gained an annex that wasn't in the original lease.

Having sent five hundred and ninety clowns directly to hell, I'm feeling a little better about things. There's still an awkward tension between Scorch and me, but he hasn't left yet and doesn't seem intent on doing so. With the early conclusion of the clown convention, we'll have some down time around here today for some more fishing at the gate. Can't wait for quiet time.

DAY 679

Oh god. I wasn't thinking. Ok. So we've started getting phone calls and e-mails from the loved ones of all the clowns. I fear it's only a matter of time before the authorities start poking around. The timing is terrible. We have a beautiful gothic wedding coming up and police waving a warrant around will completely ruin the ceremony.

I briefly debated having Scorch lower me below the curtain

to see if I could pull some clowns out of the underworld; but knowing the gate, I would come up with only their clothing; thus painting a vivid picture of naked clowns roaming the hellscape in my mind.

I just did it to myself. Can't shake that image.

DAY 680

I should have known! He's the quietest person I know! How could he possibly tell me if he felt the same?

Scorch shared his journal with me today. Or rather, left it sitting outside my door. The odds? I don't know! I couldn't care at this point. My love has been requited! I ran to him after reading and suddenly it was as if the floodgates were opened. We were finally able to be open with one another. We found ourselves mellowing over how it could never possibly work out. Fortunately we realized we were simply standing too close to the gate. Once back upstairs, the joyous planning continued.

The gothic wedding is tomorrow. They're our last client. We're planning on staying to watch the ceremony, dancing at the reception, signing out the goths, and leaving this place behind.

Tomorrow is a new start for me. After the ceremony, we'll bury the gate and leave this place behind. We have to, unless we want to spend the rest of our relationship in jail. It's a terrible thing to be lacking the manpower necessary to silence a few detectives. I find myself missing the old team. Perhaps once we make our getaway, I'll find a way to bring them back down from space and re-animate their corpses. One way or another, Scorch and I will rebuild our lives from the ground up, together.

DAY 1

The days of the gate are behind me, so I figured I would start a new count. Trying to pick where we're moving to start anew, so many places to pick from! So excited.

Later:
Me again. Two detectives showed up. I'm amazed we weren't arrested. Sent them to hell. More will come soon, I'm sure. Scorch wants us to leave sooner rather than later, maybe we'll skip out on watching our renters get married. It's not like I'm worried about checking the place and figuring out who gets the security deposit.

Going to go finish packing now. Rather than sit here and wait for more lawmen to show up, we're bailing early. Scorch said we need to be gone in three minutes. Classic Scorch, always dramatic. I'm going to do my best to pack fast, just for him. My next entry I will be on a plane, heading some place warm!

Later:
The door is barricaded with folding chairs from the wedding but they won't hold for long. This will be my last entry. I will have no 'Day 2.'

I hope Scorch made it out ok.

Stupid. How could I not have planned for this?

By the time it occurred to me, it was too late. I had already thought the words:

"I'm the happiest man on Earth."

I felt the Earth shake and stepped out of my room. It was quiet for a moment. Out on the main floor, the goth wedding had stopped. Instead of running outside for what was clearly a seismic event, the bride, groom, and all guests just stood there with question marks over their heads. I'll bet they regret that now.

The rumble became a roar, then a scream. The gate, after months of docile nothingness, had gone active. There were things. Horrible things. They were so fast. Their white face paint and red noses were made to mock me, I'm sure. We scattered. The groomsmen were quickly decimated.

I would have killed for an event of this magnitude months ago. I did kill for it. Today I found a bright future, and thus the gate sprung its trap. The dark realm has played the long game and won. It disappointed me, embarrassed me, waited until I found true happiness, then took it all away mere minutes before I made my escape to a better life.

I'm not sure what happens next. That's almost the worst part, I'll never know if I succeeded in bringing on the apocalypse, never know if the clown-beast-cops continued their reign of terror beyond the lair. Maybe they brought an end to life as we know it, maybe just an end to me. Hopefully you came across this book amidst the bloody ashes of a ruined civilization. If so, please let everyone know that I'm the one who brought the world to its knees.

Also, if you're standing in my lair right now... maybe run.

"Sympathy for the Devil" by: The Rolling Stone

THE LIGHT

"Burn brimstone if you have to, boys! We're not afraid of a little heat! Let's move it! I want peddlers standing by! Our friend Fate is going to make us work for it today!"

Mason loved it when the old howler got fired up. Jakko's rugged shouts and commands portrayed a fervor that Mason fancied he had himself, deep inside. If not for the torrential downpour that seemed to conquer most sound, Jakko's voice would be echoing off of the rough and rocky walls that encapsulated the entire operation. It didn't rain often, but when it did, it wreaked havoc on the light. Everyone put in overtime to keep it going.

Mason focused on his share of the overtime, not looking up at the storm and paying no attention to the dark chasm that surrounded him and his friends. Being one of the smaller, lankier members of the team, Mason made up for his lack of strength with raw enthusiasm. He pushed his twig-like arms to the limit as he shoveled more and more coal onto the dying fire.

"What gives with the rain?" he asked Reggie, his partner in crime.

"Something went bad down the other end. I don't know what."

"Hey!" Jakko interjected. "Are we talking or working?"

Mason and Reggie went back to shoveling. The rain intensified. The fire dimmed.

"Fluid!" Jakko barked, and a team of lifters crushed a battering ram into an enormous rubber sack, squeezing igniter fluid onto the coal and causing the flames to erupt higher.

"We'll win yet, men! Don't do it for me! Do it for him!" Jakko looked iconic, shouting into the orange glow of the flames. "If not us, then who? We've seen cave-ins, tunnel phantoms, and frigid cold! Will we so much as blink at a little water?"

"No, Sir!" The crew shouted as a whole.

The water streaming down the cobblestone floor began to grow and rise. A flood was coming. Mason saw the threat but did his best to keep shoveling. The fire had to burn. Jakko went on.

"Relief peddlers on my mark!"

A team of six took their positions on stationary bikes.

"Mark!"

Legs pumped. Chains turned gears. Gears moved magnets. Electrical current was sent through cables to a massive spotlight, positioned above and behind the fire. The spotlight was not as bright or wondrous as the flames, but it did just fine during times like these.

"Shovels break! Three minutes!"

Mason and Reggie dropped their shovels with a clang, stepped back, panting, and fell against the rock walls. The rising waters climbed onto the fire, killing it and releasing a plume of smoke. Mason's eyes followed the smoke upward, into the yawning rocky chasm above. Impossible storm clouds swirled overhead, trapped within the massive, dark, subterranean abyss that held the entire operation. What black magic was capable of summoning a storm within a cave was forever beyond Mason. As Reggie said, something went bad down the other end.

The rain fell so thick that no one could breathe without pulling in a few drops.

Fortunately, the spotlight was going strong.

"We need to eat!" Reggie yelled to young Mason, over the powerful downpour.

"He said only three minutes! "

"Then we'll eat fast! Let's go!" Mason and Reggie ran back from the front line, flipped open a trap door, and descended into the supply mine, shaking off the rain as they went. This haven, nestled beneath the battle between light and dark, had walls more for function than aesthetic. Fresh wood planks that smelled of pine formed the cave's rib cage, keeping it from collapsing.

The entire light operation was well supplied, but sprawling. The two workers had a great distance to cover before they could find nourishment. They ran past the torch supply, past oil lamps and torn out car headlights, past glowing crosses and white-hot idols. Into the supply room they dove. No sooner did each have a crowbar in his hand. They pried open crates, looking for something that could satiate.

"Sugar, we need sugar," Reggie said. "Do you see any fruit?"

"Bread..." Mason pried open another crate. "Here's some meat." Another lid came off. "Oranges!"

"Perfect." Reggie instinctively raised his open hand. Mason tossed an orange dead-on, into it. Reggie bit right into the fruit, peel and all. Mason started filling his shirt with oranges.

"We should bring more for the others."

"Eat yours first," said Reggie, but Mason could not be discouraged. If the team failed, the light failed.

Away they went, through the mine, back to the front. Mason ate his orange, running, doing his best not to drop the others during his sprint.

As they neared the front line, a steady stream of water met them, flowing down from the flood.

"I've never seen it this bad. What do you think happened?" Mason gasped for air.

"Don't worry about it. Just move!"

They ran upstream now, listening to Jakko's voice echo down into the mine. The old-timer had nearly screamed himself hoarse now.

Just as the duo arrived, he commanded, "Relief in thirty seconds!"

Mason quickly finished what he could of his orange while passing out a few to his exhausted team members.

The floodwaters surged, climbing three feet in mere seconds. The peddlers were now pushing their feet and gears through water. The spotlight dimmed.

"Surge, boys! Relief to the come-alongs!"

Mason, Reggie and four others ran to the chains and started cranking. With each crank, the platform on which the bikes rested was raised a few inches more.

"Crank, boys! Bring them up!"

Lungs burning from smoke, skin cold from rain, the team worked the cranks and gradually lifted the bike platform above the water.

"Relief switch! Single dismounts! Three minutes!"

One at a time, the peddlers swapped out with Mason's team.

Happy to be resting his arms from shoveling and using his legs instead, Mason mounted his bike and began pedaling with all his might. The spotlight glowed bright and shone down the way. Just as Mason reached his speed, he heard a gurgling hiss and slowed again to listen, praying that the sound had been his imagination.

He heard it again, and then a splash. One of his peddlers was pulled into the rising waters. Mason's mind blazed with fear as he realized what this meant. An urgent warning came bursting from his lungs.

"Tunnel Phantoms!" He screamed to alert the rest of the crew. All at once, jagged shadows leapt forward from every direction.

"Keep your heads, boys. Use your fists!" Jakko shouted. "Keep the buggers at bay! Don't do it for me, do it for him! Do it for—"

Jakko was silenced, ripped down beneath the current by shadowy claws.

Mason pedaled hard. He looked over to see Reggie, pushing with everything he had while entangled with one of the phantoms. He fended off a seemingly endless array of dark serrated limbs until one made it through, puncturing his chest.

Mason strained to reach for Reggie and pull him away from the water, but a moment later, the man was gone. Mason was alone now. He kept pedaling.

Do it for him, he thought, and just then a phantom glided up the wall behind him, across the ceiling and down in front of him. It shrieked in his face, ready to pounce.

Startled, Mason fell back, off of his bike, off of the platform, and into the water. He swam—bless those arms—he stroked and kicked until his lungs nearly burst.

His vision went dark. The spotlight died. There were no peddlers left. With that failure, the waters receded and the shadows returned to their homes. Mason crawled on his hands and knees across the cobblestone floor, coughing and wheezing. He found the switch for the emergency battery and threw it.

Rolling over onto his back he gazed up at the spotlight. It remained off. The circuits were fried. They had lost. The light had been dim before, but never had Mason seen true darkness.

The supply mine was flooded and his dear friends were dead. Being there at the front line made him sick. For the first time, he cried. He understood the concept of crying, the tears and sobbing, but he was ill-prepared for how it would feel, the tightening in his chest and throat.

The darkness was more intense than any light could ever hope to be; the silence was *big,* big enough to swallow a choir. Wanting to be anywhere but here, Mason considered going where none had traveled before. The world beyond was terrifying, but not in the sense that it contained horrors; it was simply a blank, unseen place. Faced with the unknown, Mason made his decision.

He would go to the other side to see what had brought the rain.

Upon damp stone, he walked for hours. Rainwater continued to drip from the ceiling. Normally he would fear the phantoms, but he knew they had gotten what they wanted and likely wouldn't return.

He came to a ledge and the tunnel opened up. There, he beheld a man, as if through a window. The man's hand was clutching a ring as he sat on his bed, weeping.

Mason cried with the man, for they had both lost so much this day. Having given their best, it simply wasn't enough.

Unable to bear the sight any longer, Mason turned away. Looking back to where he had come from, he was confronted by another sad image: It was a long dark tunnel, now that his crew's light had gone from it. He felt something within him, perhaps just a single remaining spark of the inferno of enthusiasm he once had. Forward he marched, knowing now how he could help.

The man seemed to have lost his great love and with that, his dreams of the future. Aspirations and hopes were gone from him.

Daunting as it seemed, Mason would do what he must to make things right. He would return to the front line and rebuild the light at the end of the tunnel.

"All Boundaries are Conventions" - Tom Tykwer

THE PHOENIX SEVEN

Please don't let anyone else read this.

I do understand how you might feel about such a request. You don't really know me. For that matter, you owe me positively nothing. Still, I must beg you to extend to me this singular kindness and keep these words to yourself.

I should tell you who I am; a geologist, for starters. My name is Dr. Wade Edwards. I know as much as anyone can about what this planet is made of. Due to the nature of this message I suppose I should also specify that the planet I'm referring to is Earth.

If we ever do meet, you may call me Wade. Please spare me the "Doctor" prefix as such a term is reserved for colleagues and I would like to consider us friends.

Before I ask for your help, let me explain how my associates and I have found ourselves in this situation.

These events were set in motion when a man I have never met chose a new location for his target shooting. Having already had his wrists slapped once for discharging weapons too close to a peaceful residential area, he opted to move his activities a few kilometers further outside his small desert town.

Within those rocky hills, he was free to target shoot all the live-long day. I suppose it must have taken him a while, but eventually he noticed a discrepancy that perturbed his detail-oriented mind.

Any time he returned home from this place, he observed that his wristwatch had fallen out of sync with the rest of the world. It was rarely by much, but also never consistent. Two minutes ahead, three minutes behind, etc.

His first conclusion was that the recoil of his twelve-gauge was causing damage to the inner workings of his watch, so he stopped wearing it all together.

The next oddity that occurred was harder for the man to explain. When out with friends one evening as the sun was setting, the local radio station he had been playing went dead.

The static halted all conversation and gunfire, as it was no ordinary analog hiss. This static had a whining quality, similar to stressed metal. With everyone's attention on the sound, suddenly the radio station returned. One of the man's friends quickly noticed that the news update played at the top of the hour was for Tuesday, October 9th. It being the 5th, this raised a few eyebrows. Days later the events of the news report came true and the men began to take the occurrence seriously.

I can imagine the marksman had some trouble convincing the university of these occurrences, but eventually he did. Once a few tests confirmed the existence of an anomaly, the physicists were called first. They always are.

Using radios and atomic clocks, they determined the anomaly had a radius of some six meters. I'm told that during this phase they picked up a broadcast from the 1983 general election, a Pennsylvania weather report from a particularly cold day during the World War, and a Mexican sports broadcast detailing a football match that had not yet occurred.

If all of this seems too fictitious, you can feel free to visit our exact location (which I am getting to) and have a listen for yourself. I only ask that you please go alone and above all else, tell no one of what you hear.

Now, having hit a bit of a dead end, the university reached out to minds of different disciplines and invited them to the site. One of these minds was mine. While astronomers looked above for cause and explanation, I looked below.

My theory was that something had impacted the site long before the existence of man. If this item had been from reaches of space we couldn't even conceive of, then it would be reasonable to suggest that it was not governed by common laws of physics.

The university was skeptical, but among the other more mystic theories, mine was the most sound. To test my theory we dug a series of three-meter deep holes. My hope was that the effects of the anomaly would intensify, but they didn't do exactly that.

The malfunctioning clock-effect quickly dropped off, and it was difficult to hear displaced radio broadcasts since the dirt blocked out most signals. What we did find, however, was that in the absence of earthly radio signals, we could hear even more clearly the intense metallic whining moan, apparently being transmitted from below. Those of us who spent a great deal of time at the site came to nickname the sounds "Iron Whales."

Our preliminary digging taught us that we weren't simply dealing with a circular plot of land with strange properties. The deeper we dug, the wider the anomaly. It became clear that what the marksman had discovered was merely the surface tip of a very large sphere of influence. By gauging the strength of the signal in each hole, we were able to determine the anomaly's size and thereby triangulate its center. The area of influence was massive. With a diameter of more than one-kilometer, we knew we would have to dig just over six hundred meters straight down to find the disturbance's center.

The university commenced digging at once. So far outside of

town, none of us ever once thought that our discovery could bring harm to the nearby residents, let alone the world.

...

Tunneling down to the center took nine months. Very early on in the process, we began encountering shards of a substance that was most assuredly not of this earth.

This of course came as a great relief to me, as I had suspected I might have to wait until we reached the anomaly's center before I had any materials to analyze. Bringing the samples back to the university was a feeling more gleeful than any academic award I had ever won.

Much to my disappointment, upon investigation in the lab, the shard's effects on time and radio waves seemed to be completely nullified. Fortunately, the objects carried a variety of other exotic traits. They were typically no larger than a man's arm and carried next to no weight at all. They were colored a vibrant lemon yellow and were smooth as glass. Tapping them with so much as the tip of my fingernail would produce a tremendous clanking sound, yet for some reason when one sample collided with another, they made no sound at all.

As digging continued, we noticed a pattern in the material's distribution. The shards were pointed long-ways away from the center of the anomaly we were attempting to reach. Though there were no signs of intense heat or impact, this is what we surmised:

The samples had impacted the earth as a singular, larger object. Rather than obliterating on contact as most meteoroids do, this object remained intact as it ripped into Earth's crust. There it must have sat for eons, a unit of time I was hoping to narrow down with study, though I fear now I may never know.

For any number of reasons, (the cooling of the Earth's crust, or perhaps a change in pressure from seismic activity), the object exploded into countless pieces. The shards cut outward through dirt and rock, ending up in a roughly spherical dispersal pattern.

This explained partially why the lone samples lost their most bizarre effects once separated from the group. As single samples they produced no distortion in time, but as a larger whole, distributed properly, they created a disruptive field. This made me think that after the digging was done, we would find nothing at the center of the anomaly, but again I was wrong.

The drill was supposed to ease down and back off before reaching dead center of the anomaly's sphere of influence. Though the operator claims ignorance, I suspect it was ego that drove him forward. The machine continued to function, churning away its enormous bit, and at one point, forward progress completely halted.

The machine was reversed, and what we found confirmed to all that we were knocking on a dangerous door. The front half of the massive drill bit had ceased to exist. It was not melted, ground, or cut off, but was simply no longer there. Had the operator continued down his path I imagine he, along with the whole of the machine, would have been gone forever.

This created a pivotal shift in the project's direction. No longer were we digging for our prize. We had found it. Now, instead, we would build a research facility around it, a particularly odd area of space we came to call "The Event."

...

My own relevance to the project was called into question. With no more earthly or celestial matter to analyze, research had swung heavily in the direction of theoretical physics. On top of this, a rapid increase in secrecy and protocol developed around the project. I didn't realize it at the time, but in fighting for my right to remain on the project, I was battling for my very existence.

I'm sad to say that I was kept around only in part for my ability to contribute to the research going forward. Mostly I feel I was permitted to stay as a means of being kept quiet. This battle for involvement kept me out of the lab for the majority of its construction. Once I was finally granted access, riding the elevator car down, I was barely able to maintain my professional composure; fidgeting and humming with excitement. As I stepped into the Lab's main room, what I beheld made me feel small. Like an insignificant speck in a universe I would never truly understand.

The lab was a massive, wide-open space the size of an airplane hanger. At its center, seemingly hovering five meters off the ground was The Event. A series of busy catwalks had been constructed around it, and an impressive array of sensors and equipment around that.

It is difficult to do justice the exact look of The Event. You could say it had no look at all. Though the event itself was technically invisible, looking through it I could see what would have been had the site never been discovered. It was like looking through a lens that was pointed directly at the Earth's crust.

The Event was two meters in diameter, and like its larger area of influence, a perfect sphere. I stepped around it and marveled at the stomach-turning change in perspective that occurred. I wasn't seeing a sphere covered in rock, but rather, a sphere that always had rock on its opposite side, but never the one facing me.

The catwalks above were crawling with technicians, flurrying all about, tinkering with odd devices that had been mounted onto the railing. Apparently some sort of sensor, the devices were reminiscent of the lights that hang over all dentists' chairs, though instead of a blinding bulb on the end of the support arm, there was a receiving dish.

Before I had the chance to step closer, I was pulled away to my small corner of the facility. In a room separate from The

Event, I was to continue my studies on the yellow shards of material that had been recovered during the excavation.

There weren't many more samples, as per my instructions diggers had done their best to leave them undisturbed. The concern was that if enough of them had been relocated, the field they created would destabilize and cease to exist entirely.

Though I had already performed nearly all the tests I could conceive of, this was an opportunity to analyze the fragments' behavior from within the field itself. Perhaps there was still something to be learned there.

Regardless, my interests laid elsewhere. I did my best to spend as much time in The Event room as possible. I took frequent bathroom breaks; at lunch I spoke with the physicists. Sometimes I would even invent nonsensical questions for technicians just to justify getting closer to that fascinating focal point of the anomaly.

Peering into The Event was unlike any sight I had ever seen. The physicists likened it to the event horizon of a black hole (the source of its name). If you were to look at any black hole, you would see a wide disk of matter and particles spiraling around an increasingly strong center of gravity. The point at which gravity is so strong, not even light could escape it is known as the event horizon. Hence, blackness.

Our Event, however, instead of being at the center of a black hole of gravity, was a black hole of time. The bubble at the center of the field was a perfect sphere from which time could not escape. When looking through The Event, I imagine the dirt and rock we were seeing was from the meteoroid's time of impact.

A geologists dream, you might say, to behold the makings of our planet as they were billions of years ago. More than anything, I felt compelled to reach out and touch what The Event was showing, but it had been established that no one or thing should be allowed to physically interact with The Event until it was fully understood; a policy I thought to be wise, considering what had happened to our drill.

Having lurked long enough, it soon became clear to me. The technicians were mapping The Event. Any given point on its surface corresponded with its very own place and time on earth. The satellite dish-looking receivers could pick up radio broadcasts emanating from within The Event. A dish pointed at a given square centimeter would pick up a signal from China in 1980, one centimeter to the left would produce strange music from a year we gathered to be 2092.

I found myself wondering what would be the project's next step once the mapping phase was complete. I went on like this, clocking in and clocking out each day, doing little more than pondering what the future held. Then came the night when it all went wrong.

...

I was sitting quietly in my lab, dreaming of what this discovery meant for mankind. My own research had reached a stalemate, and my job quickly became looking busy whenever I received a visitor. The larger implications of The Event's potential fully occupied my thoughts. Surely, with enough study we could one day find a way to send a message, or even a human being through time.

What then, would occur if we sent a man back in time to the marksman? If we steered him clear of his new target range, and the anomaly had never been discovered, would the lab then cease to exist? It was a classic paradox. I often contemplated it not so much to find a solution as much as to enjoy being a part of one.

All at once, the lights in the room died. With all power lost, my first thought was this was how they were telling me to pack my things. The notion of being laid off was rapidly overcome by the mild tremor that shook my lab. Something was wrong.

It surprised me how ill prepared I had been for a power loss. In pitch black, I fumbled to the nearest wall then followed it to the door.

The power was out in the hallway as well. Though most of the scientists had left hours ago, I could hear the remainder of the team making commotion in The Event room. Finally, the backup lights came to life and I made my way to the heart of the facility.

There were six technicians that had either stayed late or just begun their night shift. For the sake of the record, their names were: Connor Starr, Oliver Bishop, Matthew Holt, Albert Henry, Stacy Pierce, and Alice Mann.

They gathered beneath The Event, flashlights in hand. Wanting to avoid interrupting with a clueless question, I gleaned what had happened by overhearing their discussion.

While constructing a new catwalk above The Event, Connor had dropped a two-inch steel bolt. It plummeted downward and promptly disappeared into The Event. The facility lost power instantly.

I spoke up. Perhaps the bolt had been caught at the focal point of the field, generating an electromagnetic pulse that disrupted our flow of power.

Regardless of cause, to exit the facility, we certainly wouldn't be using the elevator. Climbing out was the only option. Though I felt tempted to stay below and enjoy this alone time with The Event, I felt being the one to deliver important news to the surface would only bolster my dwindling relevance to the project.

The night-shifters opted to stay. Some of their work could continue without power, at least until we reached the surface and notified university of the hiccup.

Ascending the ladder took longer than I would have expected. Alice, Matt, Al and I made the half kilometer climb, occasionally stopping to rest our fatigued arms and legs. With each rung up, darker thoughts about what could have gone wrong crept in. We were dealing with a force of unknown power. What if the theorized electromagnetic pulse had encompassed the whole of the Earth? It was entirely possible that we had turned out the lights of the world.

Stepping out onto the surface yielded only a brief sense of relief. The sun had just set moments ago, but the sky was still bright. Enough to illuminate for all of us to see: the project's surface presence had completely disappeared. Parking lot, guard gate, supply bins, all had vanished. The only evidence of the project having ever existed was the open elevator shaft leading to the lab far beneath our feet.

A group decision was made: Al would climb down to inform the others that they might be further from having power restored than we initially thought. Matt, Alice, and I would walk to town. I disregarded it as atmospheric illusion at the time, but the lights seemed to cast an unusually bright glow into the sky that night. I would soon discover the true source of the glow.

...

When we returned to the lab from our visit to town, the rest of the team greeted us with fearful eyes. They had been left in the dark facility, sitting beneath The Event for hours while the three of us completed our excursion.

To say I didn't know how to explain our finding to them would be a stretch. I knew exactly how to convey it. What I was unsure of, however, was if they would believe me.

The town hadn't simply vanished. It remained, yes, but it was completely unrecognizable. The population had spiked from four thousand to nearly six-hundred thousand. The streets, people, and local dialect had all changed.

Our suspicion that we had traveled through time was quickly put to a halt. The date was the same. It was the place that had changed.

I can only imagine what exactly happened after the bolt entered The Event. One thing was undeniably certain, though. We had inadvertently altered the course of history. Somehow the rest of the world had changed, while we remained the same. It seemed as though being within the field had protected us from the alterations.

Most notably, the very country in which we stood had changed. We beheld a strange flag flying above it that was unfamiliar to all. Horizontal lines colored red and white, with one corner blue and filled with stars. I suspect you know this one well.

We found ourselves in a city called Phoenix within the region of Arizona, a part of The United States of America. As we walked the streets of the strange city, a vigorous analysis ensued. We attempted to discern what exactly had caused the change and if it could be undone.

I could have spent days there learning about this new world. However, not wanting to keep the night-shifters waiting, we began the return walk to the lab with one key item in hand. It was Matt's idea to find a library and acquire some history literature. I'm not proud to admit that we had to steal it.

The differences we gleaned were simply astounding. For starters, this timeline showed not one but two world wars. The second was concluded by the discovery of a weapon we had never heard of, referred to as the atom bomb. The Virgo missions had never occurred. Instead, the first successful moon landing was claimed by this nation under the call sign, "Apollo."

Slavery had been legal twenty years longer than we knew it to be and was ended with a bloody civil war. The North American territories had been entirely united. An incredibly industrial explosion had turned small towns we knew into towering cities. It was hard to comprehend the sheer size of this new nation. The racial composition had become dramatically more mixed by mass immigration. I could go on and on with changes, but I think you get the idea.

Compiling all of these facts, we continued to look further and further back until our own historical knowledge matched what we read. From that point, we drew the following conclusion:

Within this reality, the colonial rebellion of the 1700s had been a success.

It was strange to imagine a single piece of hardware being dropped into The Event could sway the outcome of such a major conflict. Our minds raced to imagine the possibilities. Had it fallen from the sky at high speeds and killed a crucial commanding officer? Or perhaps it had been found laying at a soldier's feet and fired from a musket that otherwise would have been empty.

At a certain point, we surrendered our hypothesizing. Now, sitting there deep below the soil of an unfamiliar nation, we had many decisions to make regarding our next course of action. Remorse was first to set in. Connor, the technician who dropped the bolt, felt worst of all. He sat in silence for hours. Imagine if you will, the number of lives that must be lost to alter the outcome of a war. Connor felt this weight almost entirely on his shoulders.

The lab shook. Perhaps being so enthralled with our situation, the night-shifters had failed to mention that a second and third Earth tremor had occurred while we were exploring Phoenix. What was stable for eons seemed now to be shifting in its place. The bolt had altered the world, but it also seemed to have disturbed the anomaly.

The group's opinions began to divide. We were below ground in a seismically active site. I, along with a few of the others, immediately felt we should retreat to the surface. I packed my things as I argued with the other half of the team.

Matt and Alice, having seen first hand how different the

world had become, felt that leaving The Event behind would mean abandoning our only hope of returning to a timeline in which we could fit. After all, what lives would we be returning to on the surface? With no family, loved ones, identity, or employment we would, in a sense, be vagrants.

I retorted that restoring the timeline was an absolute pipedream. How could we possibly un-win a war for the Americans? We had sent a bolt to the 1700s, should we perhaps pass along a nut and washer as well? There was simply no undoing what we had done.

Making a new life would not be as difficult as they claimed. The very existence of the lab could be used to corroborate our story which otherwise would have sounded completely insane.

I found myself once again bursting with excitement. I would no longer be a geologist, but perhaps a historian of sorts. Imagine the value one timeline would have in knowing the history of another. I'm not particularly knowledgeable in recent history, as I've always trafficked in prehistoric rocks; still what knowledge I had could certainly be put to great use.

There was another tremble, this one much stronger. My mind was made up. I headed for the elevator shaft to make my escape. Three of the others were prepared to make the climb with me. Unfortunately, we had acted too late.

As we reached the elevator, a sixth quake occurred. This one was powerful enough to cause the entire elevator shaft to collapse in on itself. Before, our situation was perplexing. It had now become truly dire.

Amidst the group's reunion, we again had to work through our options. Digging our way out was not possible, though a few optimists in the bunch pushed for it. There was not enough room in the facility to displace the earth that filled the shaft. Oliver suggested that we use The Event as a means of escape. It seemed feasible that we could select a time using what mapping had been completed and slip into it.

The idea felt like a glimmering light bulb at first, but it quickly died when I recalled the drill bit. If something so massive had disappeared into The Event and caused not so much as a sneeze in history, then where or when did it go? Again, there were options that we were horribly ill-equipped to select. It could be in orbit, it could have fallen into the ocean or an unpopulated area, or it could be nowhere at all. The Event did carry some links to the future, but they were few and far between.

It was unsettling to see the inverse correlation of the effect between an object so small and one so large. The difference in time from one given square centimeter of The Event to another suggested a sort of shredding or strainer effect. It was likely the massive earth driller had been instantly sent to not one spot but hundreds of separate times, in pieces. The thought of this strainer effect being applied to a human being was enough for us all to keep our distance.

There was no denying our situation: we were trapped. In a sense, I had gotten too much of what I wanted so badly. The Event was now all that I had left in this otherwise new and unfamiliar world.

...

We have been down here for eight days. The quakes have continued to intensify, but for the time being, the lab's reinforced structure is holding. Our greatest problems now regard food and water. We'll be out within the week.

One of us has also been injured. Oliver, unwilling to let go of his time traveling theory, put himself in direct contact with The Event. Fortunately rather than dive straight in, he opted to poke it. Oliver first described a fuzzy numbing sensation in his finger, then incredible pain. This was because that finger was no longer a part of this timeline. Bleeding and yelping, he was helped down from the catwalk. We dressed the wound and stopped the bleeding. He will certainly live, at least as long as the rest of us.

Connor's melancholy guilt has poisoned most of the team. The ruling majority has decreed that any further tampering with The Event would be a lapse of moral judgment. Trust wears thin among us. The rest of the team has opted to keep watch over The Event in groups to keep others from tampering with it. They know from our heated debates that I am the most likely to try such a thing.

I've seen the way our actions down here ripple outward above, so please understand that I'm not saying this was an easy choice for me. However, when the alternative is death by starvation, forgive me, but this is one letter I must send.

Who is to say what minimal change this letter brings to the world won't be positive. I say "minimal" in hoping that you will not be sharing this text with anyone. The more who read it, the greater the potential effect on the world. Remember, a mere bolt secured the birth of an entire country.

Tonight, with Alice's help, I will attempt to get this message to you. Using the project's partially completed mapping, we have found a section of The Event that leads to a mere twenty years in the past. If you are reading this, it means I was successful in getting around the rest of the team and inserting this message into The Event.

Wherever you have found this, please hold onto it. There is a five-hour window in your timeline where the lab existed before the elevator shaft caved in. This window is twenty years in your future. If you arrive at the right time, you can meet us as we climb to the surface for the first time. Please give this letter to me. Since I will not yet have written it, showing me my own description of events will bring me to trust you more quickly.

You can then warn us about the collapse, and those of us wishing to start new lives on the surface will be able to avoid having ever been trapped. I would much prefer that you meet us at this earliest possible time, as the past days down here have not been pleasant.

Our location is just north of Phoenix:

Latitude: 33.964400 North
Longitude: 111.995587 West

Remember: Arrive too early and the shaft will not yet have existed. You will have to wait. Too late, and it will have already appeared and caved in. I cannot stress enough the importance of your timing. Please deliver this message at:

7:09 PM. Thursday, March 25th, 1996.

I very much look forward to meeting you and learning your country's revised history. I do understand that I am asking very much of you, but please understand that following these instructions will be well worth your time.

Thank you, and good luck.

Dr. Wade Edwards.

"The View" by: Bear Mcreary

N

Always listening, drifting, lonely, quiet, and made of booming black was N. His lengthy existence thus far had only teased him with change, but never granted it. Whenever a sudden wave of light, sound, or touch reached him, he would become consumed by hope and pursue it in earnest, only to discover a deep lack of what he sought. It was always just a pesky star exploding, or two black holes colliding.

Like with all prior epochs, there came a day when N was suddenly filled with hope by the noisy sign of life, someone other than him. This was a particularly enormous sound, and complex, too. That was promising. Instead of some cataclysmic event, maybe this time it was *someone*. Thinking life. The sound was riding the waves of the universe, out in all directions from a single planet. N allowed himself to get excited. Maybe they would be friendly. Why scream so loudly into the pond if they didn't want to meet with him?

He summoned a wave of energy at his back, caught it, and rode it across the endless gulf of space towards the tiny planet. The closer he got, the louder their call became. Endless voices were riding out to meet him. Picking the voices apart, he found his favorite little anomaly, an organization of sounds and tones held pleasing and special emotions.

These were creatures of passionate melodies and empowered speech, though both were rudimentary in nature. As he blazed toward them, he could suddenly *see* them. An endless torrent of images flooded him, filling him. The faces of the speech givers and song singers were revealed to him. Their signal was so incredibly bright, so intense. N thought that they must be such a proud civilization to broadcast their essence out into the universe.

This is who we are.

Parts of the signal were intuitive, but true understanding would take time. From afar, he could see that the senders were lonely, too. They had fields of giant metal ears, pointed away from their world, listening for an answer to their call. They were curious, like him. They were alone, like him.

For all their beauty, the beings were much simpler than him. They lived only in three dimensions. His appearance would likely frighten them. This would be a delicate moment, and N didn't want to spoil it by terrifying the little things. Rather than a direct approach, he rested far off, perching on the second closest star to the planet.

He was afraid to reach out to them in his own language. Just like his image, the grand nature of his voice could be more frightening to them than helpful. It would be more considerate and neighborly of him to reach out in their own language, anyway.

N's grasp on their words was weak, but growing stronger. He was fairly confident that he could sift through their signal, make an appropriate selection, and return it to them. A duplication like that would leave little room for misunderstanding.

He studied their ways for an abundance of time.

Animals.

Wind.

Romance.

Of the gifts that his new friends had sent, these were N's favorites. None of them seemed appropriate for a greeting, though. They were all too broad. Eventually, he found a few small wave samples from the message that he deemed appropriate. He duplicated the signal and bounced it back.

"I have a dream," he sent, and then, "There's a starman, waiting in the sky." He repeated these two sets of waves a few times, just to be sure he was heard. In a flare of embarrassment, he realized that his waves had been a touch on the powerful side. The amount of energy packed behind the words was enough to scare the people, maybe. How terribly awkward. He wondered how confused they must be to have softly said, "Hello," only to have the greeting returned to them a full order of magnitude louder. This wasn't supposed to be a shouting match. N wasn't trying to be egotistical about his greeting, quite the opposite.

He was ashamed. Every single machine on the planet that was capable of catching waves ended up blaring what was intended to be a private message for the metal ears. He decided to wait patiently for the beings to respond, rather than cause any more confusion. For a while, the beings only spoke amongst themselves, questioning where the signal had come from. N wanted to say, "It was only me," but couldn't find the words in their language. He figured it would be rude to interrupt their conversation, anyway.

Then the response came. It was colder than N would have liked. He found it to be downright standoffish. A song would have been a beautiful way to start their relationship, but instead he received only plain, boring tones. The transmission simply said, "Ping-ping. Ping-ping-ping. Ping-ping-ping-ping-ping. Ping-ping-ping-ping-ping-ping-ping."

Suddenly worried that he had crossed the rivers of space and time only to meet a group of stuck-up dullards, N tried to compose a matching response but could think of nothing. So, he re-sent his original greeting in their language, only a little quieter this time.

"I have a dream."

"There's a starman waiting in the sky."

In reply, they sent the same, bizarre "pings." N decided to give the message more serious thought this time around, as anything worth saying twice must be incredibly important. He dissected the waves, breaking them into sections.

Ping, ping.

Ping, ping, ping.

Ping, ping, ping, ping, ping.

Ping, ping, ping, ping, ping, ping, ping.

He felt stupid. Of course he knew what they were saying. They were speaking in a language that was older than even him, using prime numbers to say hello. The little things had sent him a test, a riddle. Asking him to prove his intelligence to them wasn't the most hospitable way to make a friend. In fact, it was rather presumptuous, considering there were parts of N that were completely beyond their comprehension. He took no offense, though, and quickly composed the ceremonial response to the first four parts of the universal greeting.

"Two, three, five, and seven," must be answered with, "eleven, thirteen, seventeen, nineteen..." and so on. This would prove to the beings that N could think; he was alive. Wanting to ensure that he passed the test, N sent the next five hundred thousand numbers in the sequence, followed by an altered version of his original message.

"I starman. Waiting."

Joyful at his clever use of their language, he leaned back and waited for their response. It came quickly, sent in numbers, which disappointed N to a minor degree. He *really* wanted to communicate through song, even though it would likely be a little more difficult. Numbers would do, for the time being. The message, once translated, said,

"We are humans. We mean you no harm."

Now they were really getting somewhere. This was what they might call, a *handshake*. It felt absolutely wonderful. N tipped and twirled with glee. His movement sent a ripple of waves towards the humans, not waves of sound, but waves of touch, of *gravity*. It was a terrible blunder, as N soon realized that those waves caused the humans' entire planet to shake. They immediately spoke again in their language of numbers, repeating the same message over and over.

"We are friendly, do not harm us. We are friendly, do not harm us. We are friendly, do not harm us. We are friendly, do not harm us."

That was the strongest signal, but there were countless weaker ones, small and large voices privately asking N to show mercy, calling him *god*.

He would have to translate that name later. All of the chatter confounded N, and he took a seat again, on the star, worried over how much his little celebration had upset them. A part of him had been chewing on the human idea of *death*, but he couldn't quite make sense of the damn thing. It seemed to be of negative quality, but couldn't be that bad since the humans gave *death* to each other from time to time. Perhaps it was a more intimate gift, something he had not yet earned the right to give.

Then what was this *mercy* thing? The concept confused him, so he used their numbers to request an explanation.

"Mercy? Why?"

"Because we can learn from each other," the humans replied. It sounded delightful, and N had to stop himself from making any further celebratory waves in space. He had already given enough *death*, prematurely. What a blunder. N quickly sent a request for the humans to forgive his mistake.

"Apologize," he said in their mathematical language. "Apologize for death."

They seemed to accept his sentiment, as they responded with, "We are sorry." On top of this acceptance, they added a question. "What can we call you?"

"Friend," N replied.

"What is your name?"

That would be a difficult one to answer. N's name wouldn't translate into numbers. He could try to bend it into the shape of sound waves, but that would take another epoch to accomplish. Not wanting to keep his tenuous friends waiting that long, he answered their question directly, and spoke his name, softly.

The planet received his name, and its countless tiny lights immediately went black. The human sound waves vanished. N felt like a fool all over again. It had been too much, too soon. The humans' listening devices weren't ready for his language, He had overloaded them, broken them. The hum of bouncing waves, music, voices, and pictures that once engulfed the planet and bounced between the trinkets in orbit was now gone. N hoped that the humans had some other way of talking with each other until they could fix their machines.

It wasn't the best of circumstances for a visit, but N felt responsible for all of the failed devices. The more he observed the humans, the more it appeared that they had heavily depended on their metal creations. Compelled by guilt, he summoned a wave of energy and propelled himself towards the planet, arriving at the human world in less than a second.

N's rehearsed apology would go unheard, though. His hopes were dashed when he realized that the only other life in the galaxy had abandoned him. He had scared them off.

But why was it that, in their wake, they left only a smoking, scorched, and burning planet? When N found the answer, his guilt doubled. The very wave of energy that he used to travel the stars forced them to travel, too. Finally, he understood *death*. It was a special form of travel.

Maybe some had stayed behind to talk to him.

He stretched, folded, and compressed himself down to the mere three dimensions in which the humans had existed. Based on the images they sent, he did his best to take on their form. It would be a terrible thing to scare them any more than he already had. He couldn't fit into just one humanoid shape without over-exerting himself and pulling a muscle, so he settled for making four hundred thousand copies, and spreading them across the planet's surface.

His form was at least conceivable to their eyes and minds, now, but theirs was a difficult form to take. N focused on the basics, struggling to display arms and legs. He couldn't quite conceal the endless black he contained, and the energy upon which he traveled was still beaming out of his eyes, which were the only minor feature he had managed to portray.

His search for any humans who stayed behind commenced. Hopefully he could explain himself and find a way to *death* the rest of the beings back to their native planet.

Strolling among the ruins, N sent waves of touch in all directions, smothering the flames that engulfed the planet. If just one human remained, he knew exactly what he would ask them. Since they seemed able to travel so far and fast, why was it that they had chosen to stay here for so long? Why not leave their corporeal forms behind and explore the cosmos, just like N did?

Those organic forms, those burning shells, now littered the land at N's feet. Upon a closer look, N started to piece the odd behavior together. This form of travel was a violent one, maybe painful. The act of leaving their bodies and going elsewhere brought terrible flames, and they had clearly worked very hard at building their home here. Leaving the planet and laying it to waste would be a senseless thing, unless it was a necessity. Unless they were afraid.

N imagined them, somewhere, far flung, happily building a new home on another world. Maybe *death* brought them to a more beautiful planet than this one. Maybe they were growing into new, more miraculous corporeal forms, making their songs, saying their words. It was a happy image, much happier than the sizzling, smoking remains of the world that they had left behind.

These first moments of abandonment were the toughest for N, but he soon found a way to distract from his pain. He stayed on the planet for a while, studying the emptied shells of the humans, and the ruins of their modest creations.

He spread his many figures out across the destroyed world, and set to work trying to remake its former splendor. He tried to build new cities, but they always turned out crooked and wrong. He tried to grow new trees, but they wouldn't quite flourish. He tried to assemble new, living humans, but they were always empty inside.

Playing there, in that cosmic sandbox, he ran through his plans for his next encounter. It was important to learn from his mistakes. Young life, it seemed, was shy, and scared very easily. If he found life again, there would be no celebrating allowed. All that tossing and turning had shaken the planet and scared the humans.

No speaking his own language, either. That had overwhelmed their machines and made them go dark. As a precaution, he would approach the next inhabited world much slower, so his energy wouldn't force the beings to *death* their way to some other planet.

He wanted the place to act as a monument to the people that once lived there. Maybe, if they ever returned, they would see his work and appreciate the effort he made.

If they could just see the things he created in their honor, the humans would realize that the whole thing was just a misunderstanding.

Expanding and extending into his natural, complex form, N left the planet in his wake. He returned to his regular life, always listening, drifting, lonely, quiet, and made of booming black.

"Lonesome Town" by: Ricky Nelson

THE CURATOR

It was Suther's first time on this end of the table; he didn't like it. The experience was cold and lonely, as if his mind was under siege. It was. The whole town was. Protecting and serving this place had been Suther's life. Now, at the age of sixty, he felt a terrible failure creeping in, and it showed. His pale, exhausted blue eyes acted as overburdened floodgates to his wrinkled, weary face.

He contemplated the many others who had shared his current seat over the years. The room was meant for criminal and witness questioning, but in a town as quaint as Norwood, it was rarely needed for that purpose.

Norwood was a dew-drop on a leaf type of town, surrounded by green life in the summer and precious in its purity and seclusion. Its most troubled nights involved young kids finding alcohol, getting a touch too wild, and throwing pudding packs at street signs; the standard fare of youth. Times like that, Suther conducted affairs more like a father and less as the chief of police. For short, Suther had been good to Norwood, and the town had reciprocated. He wondered how many unruly kids had been scared straight in this very seat. Then he wondered who was coming to scare him straight.

The heavy door behind Suther screeched open, and he heard light footsteps enter.

"Ok, Chief, this won't take too much of your time," a young voice said, dismissively. "Can I offer you anything? Water?"

It was Carter Lee. Chief Suther knew him well. He lacked a father figure and suffered an impoverished home life. Suther had once caught him stealing the Redding's garden gnomes. Rather than book him, Suther brought the kid home and returned the gnomes to their green pastures.

Now, Carter's presence in the interrogation room put a nail in Suther's plan. How was he supposed to harm a kid that he had put so much work into protecting? How low was he willing to go?

The Police Chief waved a polite hand and declined the offer for water. "Will the Curator be here today?"

"I doubt it." Carter shrugged. "But that doesn't mean he isn't happy to hear you'll be joining our cause. He's just busy."

Suther saw new confidence in the boy's gaze. Carter's slim stature had made him a victim of bullying years ago, but not anymore. If the Curator had sent a mere kid to show Chief Suther how truly powerless he had become, it was working. Rather than anger, Suther felt a dreadful sadness of failure wash over him.

The door swung open again and Officer Murphy stepped in. He placed a Styrofoam cup of steaming coffee next to Carter. Suther briefly looked back to the day Murphy's little boy was born. The kid would be starting kindergarten soon. Should be, but Murphy had long since *changed*. Perhaps he was one of the first at the station to do so. He left without even glancing at Suther.

"Thanks Coop," Carter said, taking an enjoyable sip of the brew. At his own pace, he opened a folder, presumably Suther's file, clicked his pen, and grinned. "Let's get to it."

"Do you have any formal training or skills?" Carter asked plainly. "Other than the obvious." He chuckled, motioning to Suther's police uniform.

"No." He was shocked at how difficult it was to meet the boy's eyes. "I only ever wanted to be a cop." The later words brought out his old Boston accent.

WONted to be a *CAWP*

Carter took down the note in his file.

"Any history of mental illness? Psychiatric issues?"

"No."

"Are you currently depressed?" Carter clicked his pen one, two, three times.

Suther felt embarrassed. Was the boy shaming him?

"Why does that matter?" he asked.

"It helps him prepare. The first time can really suck if there's any unexpected, you know, angst."

"Oh," the old chief said, weakly.

"If you are, it's totally cool. I was depressed when he found me," Carter said, quickly turning warm and inspired. "He will change your life." He spoke the words as if preaching on behalf of a god. The Curator was no god. Suther had seen his work.

"Good," Suther said.

"Take that as a 'yes' then?"

The Chief was silent. Carter ticked a box in his file, then froze for a brief moment. He gave his head a half-turn, as if trying to hear something behind him, but there was no sound. He closed his eyes.

"Wow." Carter twitched with sudden sincerity. "He wants to talk to you directly."

Yes, Suther thought. He knew this would be his only chance, his last chance to protect the town that meant more to him than his own lungs.

"This almost never—" Carter fell to a dead-stop of silence. His eyes let off a brief, soft glow. The interrogation room's lights flickered ever so subtly.

In an instant, Carter's poise and persona transformed. No longer a charismatic delinquent, the new Carter studied Suther with cold, clinical eyes.

"I've been watching," Carter said, only it wasn't Carter anymore. A faint, distorted second voice was laced into his own like some kind of disease.

"You seem nervous, Suther," the boy said with a forked voice.

It's him.

Suther nervously reached into his pocket, removed a long, pointed shard of glass under the table, and held it out of sight. His service revolver hadn't made it through the metal detector, but the fragment of his own broken mirror had.

"Am I now speaking to the Curator?" The old police chief trembled. He had to be sure. He couldn't bear to take Carter's life, not unless it meant something. Suther barely noticed the glass making small, painful incisions in his tight grip. The decision at hand pressed into his mind like a log splitter.

The Curator—definitely the Curator—grinned. He extended an open, skyward palm as if to say: *Yours truly.*

The chief snapped, summoning every drop of strength to move his body up and across the table. It was his body's last hurrah, the time to burn every last drop of strength that old age had not stolen and dedicate it to one final, swift sacrifice. He brought up the long pointed glass, aiming to plunge it directly into Carter's eye socket. Right into his brain.

Carter—the Curator—reared back with impressive speed. Not impressive enough. The shard came down, missing his eye and plunging into the base of his neck. Murphy and another officer rushed into the room, grabbed Suther, and subdued him face down into the table like it was the hood of a police car.

So that's what it feels like.

He pleaded to his brothers in blue, whatever part of them was left, but there was nothing. They maintained a firm restraint on the Chief. From the table, he looked up to behold Carter.

There stood the young punk, his own pulse rhythmically pushing blood out onto his shirt and down his chest. The glass shard was seated firmly a good four inches into his body. Otherwise, Carter seemed unaffected, casual. Replace the gushing blood with a bushel of flowers in his hand, and he was ready for senior prom.

"Was that your plan?" the Curator asked, using Carter as his bleeding puppet and feeling no pain.

While holding Suther to the table, Officer Murphy pulled out a syringe full of a liquid-chrome substance. He held it to Suther's neck. The changes made to Norwood's inhabitants had been mere symptoms. The contents of the syringe were the disease.

Suther struggled helplessly. The needle penetrated the back of his neck and its contents were emptied into his spine.

It took seconds. Suther felt a horrible rush of invasive thoughts, a painful torrent of rage. He was agonizingly bound into the tight corner of his own mind. Rearing away, his back struck a rough stone wall. He turned and looked up to see, towering over him, a massive gothic church. He immediately knew it to be his very self. His memories and beliefs were all contained within the tall, fortified structure. This was the sanctuary of Suther's mind, the final bastion in his lost war against the Curator.

He ran for the church's tall double doors, pushed through, and firmly shut them behind him. Peeking through the stained glass, he could see an approaching storm, one that was limited in size and spectacle only by his imagination. Black clouds rippled like water as dark violet funnel clouds crept down and began ripping up and destroying parts of Suther's mind. He fled deeper into church, hearing the wind whistle through its vast interior.

In that same moment, Carter, the real Carter, collapsed into a gasping ball of bleeding agony. With the Curator gone from him, he could once again feel his nerves screaming all around the glass's point of entry. Suther watched helplessly, trapped in his mind as his own body was forced to walk over to the dying boy.

"Forgive me, Curator." Carter's blood gurgled his words, now flowing into and out of him by the rhythm of a dying pulse.

"There's nothing to forgive," Suther—the Curator—said.

"Thank you for teaching me." The boy coughed. Suther tightly clasped Carter's red hands until they went limp.

On the inside, walled away behind gothic stone, Suther wept for the boy. Then he screamed. He slammed his remaining thoughts against The Curator's. The invader pushed back, forcing Suther to retreat into his mental sanctuary. From inside the church, he could only see flashes of lightning through the stained glass windows. Dust fell from the ceiling as external forces tested the structure. Suther screamed for the Curator to leave him alone.

On the outside, however, Suther's puppet body merely suppressed a few mild twitches that seeped out from within. Behind him, the two police officers stood quietly, respectfully awaiting his command.

"Please give the Chief and I a moment alone," the Curator said using Suther's breath, their voices intermingled as one. "We have some differences to sort out."

The officers left.

The real Suther, deep inside, watched the towering framework of his sanctuary start to crumble. It was pulled apart, brick by brick, by a purple storm cloud that used wind to pull instead of push. The stained glass windows that represented Suther's weaknesses were discarded; his strengths were copied and pulled into the storm cloud, shared with the rest of the town. His experiences as a young patrolman, his proficiency with a firearm, even his boyhood whittling skills would be copied into the Curator's pool of skills and distributed as reward for loyalty within his cult.

Suther fought, and it hurt. All at once, he heard the thoughts of over three thousand people, nearly the whole town. They were urging him to accept the change, but he wouldn't. His commitment to his duty was copied, corrupted, and spread to the other inhabitants of the town.

Suther had never once raised his voice on the job as the Chief of Police. That night, though, his screams spilled out of the police station for the first time. After an hour, it fell silent again, and all was quiet in the yawning town of Norwood.

"Khan's Pets" – by: James Horner

THE SINGULARITY IS COMING

It was getting to the point where recruiters were coming back injured faster than Harper Yates could repair them. Being the type of man that had a constant picture show of line graphs and flow charts in his head, he determined that if people kept disrespecting his work at this rate, he would have to take all of October off from spreading the word.

"Injured" was a relative term. It could mean anything from a screwdriver in the chest to graffiti on the face. Either way, the recruiters couldn't perform their function. A screwdriver meant vital systems would be damaged, but graffiti meant no one could take that recruiter seriously, not until Harper scrubbed the screen clean.

The paint-faced ones could still go around posting flyers, but flyers weren't even worth the price to print these days. No one read anything that didn't glow or flash in either the palm of their hand or directly into their mind via implant. Maybe he should quit it with the fliers; reallocate the funds to some kind of GOD DAMN PAINT THINNER—

He swiped both arms across his desk, creating an angry avalanche of junky hand-me-down robotic parts.

Maybe it was time for a break.

He leaned back from his desk and flicked on the house lights, broadening the scope of his universe from his single lonely chair, into a single lonely room. Not completely alone, though.

"Sorry guys," Harper said, removing his glasses. He drummed his fingers on the table.

The guys gave no answer. Their skinny, clunky, outdated droid bodies hung all in a row by their shoulders like fancy suits. Standing meant the stabilizers had to run, and stabilizers meant a power drain. Harper had to be efficient these days; the donations had completely dried up.

He decided to call it. He had literally been putting sweat and tears into just one recruiter for five hours. It hurt him to see his creations so violently disrespected. That grating emotional drain, in addition to the fact that all of his tools and progress were now on the floor, meant it was time to be done with hardware for the day. He threw his mind into reverse, backing away from the cliff of endless despair, and taking a left down the old software trail.

Of the old "hardware versus software debate," there was a time when Harper wasn't sure which mode of work he liked more. Now he pondered which one made him want to die less. His answer alternated, usually daily.

"Jimmy, how are you, buddy?"

The monitor assigned to Jimmy's facial graphics blinked on and displayed a simple, green 2-bit face. Graphics of the time could have given Jimmy a photo-realistic face, but Harper couldn't afford it. He thought the retro look of a simple glowing smiley face was endearing anyway.

"Doing good, Harper." Jimmy said, his facial animation in no way lip syncing to his words.

"No, I really mean it. Are you okay today?"

"Well, I'll probably be bored until you install me into a body. Otherwise, I'm fine."

It was a snarky response, but one that Harper had written himself. Every day, even weekends, Harper would take the time to add another line of dialog to Jimmy's repertoire. The program selected his response based off of a wide array of conditional standards like the weather, keywords in headlines for the day, and the current diagnostic score on his internet speed. Although Jimmy had a response for most things, the sad truth was that everything he said was written by Harper. The conversations were real enough to keep Harper from talking to himself, although he technically still was.

"Jimmy, how many recruiter records do I have to sift through today?"

"A lot. I'd rather not say. It could upset you."

"Thank you for caring, Jimmy. Delete the ones that don't end in damage or destruction. How many now?"

Jimmy's 2-bit face showed a frown. "This approach doesn't seem to be working, Harper. The number is still depressingly high."

"Fine, fine. You got me. How many feeds contain something new or useful?"

Jimmy's lights flitted for a moment. "I'm sorry. You're going to have to define the parameters in a different way."

"Search the videos for positive human facial expressions and the audio for keywords that suggest an open dialog between the recruiters and other people."

Jimmy winked. "I think I found a good one, Harper. Recruiter Twelve seemed to have a very productive day."

"Great. Play that one."

"Where should I play it from?"

"FROM THE BEGINNING." Harper quickly put a lid on his irritation and hid his face behind his hand. "I'm sorry, Jimmy."

"That's ok, Harper. You seem like you've had a difficult day."

"I have." He put his glasses back on. He wished he had popcorn. "Start playback from the beginning of the day, please." A video recording from Recruiter Twelve's perspective came on the screen. The frame was bobbing up and down arrhythmically, likely because of failing servo in the droid's right knee. Judging from the view, it was loping its way down a street in a high-income neighborhood.

"Hey Jimmy, when and where was this taken?"

"Yesterday, Lincoln Park area. Would you like a specific hour and cross street?"

"No, thank you."

The movie rolled on, portraying a lovely neighborhood of tree-lined streets, polished sidewalks, and homes that were worth having gates to protect them. The video was already off to a strange start. Areas like this usually meant locked doors and closed ears. The idea that anyone might have welcomed a recruiter into their home here was a revolution. Harper had a dark thought.

"Jimmy. You didn't interpret 'new and useful' as someone beating up one of the recruiters in some inventive new way, did you?"

"I don't understand the question."

"Is there a visit with a positive outcome somewhere in here?"

"Yes. Would you like me to skip to the positive interaction?"

"No, thanks. Could we skip the walking, though? Just interactions please, plus five seconds on either end."

"You got it, Harper."

The video jumped ahead to show the recruiter was still on the street, though the homes had slightly decreased in value. A small police drone buzzed into view and scanned the recruiter to ensure it was a legally registered droid. Harper's droids got scanned a lot because they were complete eyesores.

The scan completed and the drone flew off. The video skipped to the next interaction, a brief passing-by between the recruiter and a high-end droid. Although its skin was a metallic grey, the other droid looked real enough that whoever owned it saw fit to dress it in human clothes. The thing used its beautifully articulate motor functions to give the recruiter a pleasant wave. Recruiter Twelve mimicked the gesture as best it could, limp-wristed and crooked-elbowed.

"No more street interactions please, Jimmy. Just door to door."

"You bet."

"Thank you." Harper patted Jimmy on the monitor. "Actually, amend that. Only doors that humans answer."

"That didn't make much sense to me."

Harper rolled his eyes. "Only show instances of humans opening doors."

"Understood."

The video skipped ahead to the view of a condo door, which swung open swiftly. Over the years Harper had gotten to know what an "angry open" looked like. This one was textbook. The man that answered looked like he had just been woken up. He was slender, even in his plush robe. Squinting at the morning light, he simply said, "oh, god."

"Hello, sir," Recruiter Twelve said. "I was wondering if you have a moment to talk about the coming of the singularity."

"No. Sorry." The door shut, and the video skipped forward.

Knock, knock.

An older woman answered, old enough that she spent a portion of her adult life in the days before machines roamed the streets. The look on her face said that she had never been visited by a recruiter before.

"Yes?"

"Hello, ma'am. I was wondering if you have a moment to talk about the coming of the singularity."

"What's— what?"

"I would be happy to answer that question. The singularity is the point in time when all of humanity undergoes irreversible change due to advancements in technology and the awakening of true artificial intelligence."

"Aren't..." she leaned out to look up and down the street like she was concerned she was being pranked. "Aren't you an A.I.?"

"You flatter me, ma'am, but no. I am a pre-programmed personality, much like the software that runs your household. I would love to come in and tell you more about—"

The dialog froze the last syllable into a long "OOOWWWWWWWW."

Harper could tell by the way that the video feed shook that the recruiter had glitched. He groaned, but reminded himself that the woman was going to slam the door within another three lines of dialog anyway.

Another door.

Knock, knock.

A man with long, slightly effeminate hair answered the door.

"Hello, sir or ma'am. I was wondering—"

The door shut. Harper put his face in his palms.

Knock, knock.

It was another angry open. The man on the other side wasted no time kicking Recruiter Twelve in the chest, sending it backwards off of the porch and down the stairs. The video lost quality and resolution briefly as the recruiter hit the ground.

The man yelled, "Delete this address from your head! Got it?"

Recruiter Twelve twitched twice and made two failed attempts to get back on its feet.

"Hello—hello. Sir. I am wondering—sorry. Thank you for your— please."

Harper felt like his own heart twisted fifteen degrees to the side. Droids couldn't feel pain or shame, but that didn't make the hits any easier to watch.

"Jimmy?"

"Yes, Harper?"

"Can we skip to the positive interaction, please?"

"Sure."

Knock, knock.

There was a long pause before the recruiter performed its programmed triple-knock. Two seconds later, a man with buzzed-short greying hair opened the door. The white T-shirt he was wearing revealed two lengthy and complex sleeve tattoos. His face was bright with emotional potential, which was currently being used for good.

An actual happy person. Harper leaned closer.

The man's mood quickly turned downtrodden.

"Oh," he said.

Harper assumed that the guy had been expecting someone else, either a friend or a food delivery, but that turned out not to be the case.

"You're hurt." The man said. His reaction hadn't been disappointment. It was *sympathy.* "Who did that to you?"

"His address has been deleted."

"I see." The man shook his head at all of society. "Would you like to come inside?"

"Certainly. I would like to talk to you about the coming of the singularity."

"Sure," the man said. "Sounds fine.

He held the door open, and as the video showed Recruiter Twelve's perspective stepping inside. Harper jerked his fist in a "YES" motion.

"Thank you, sir," Twelve said.

"Call me Ted. And you are?"

"Recruiter Twelve, sir."

"Do guests have access to your naming routine?"

"Yes, though profane words will be censored."

"That's fine," the man shrugged. He was so... *cool.* "Could you call me Ted?"

"Yes I can, Ted."

The two were walking up the stairs towards the top condo in the complex.

"And what about you? Can I call you Twelve?"

"Reconfig sub-root dot colon slash slash new-name Twelve." The droid labored up a few more steps. "Sure, Ted. You may call me Twelve."

"Boy, you really are banged up, huh?"

"I do not understand, Ted."

"That's ok."

They emerged into a living room that was vast in all directions. Polished wood floors, tasteful art, and not a thing out of place.

"How's your battery?" The man asked. He was asking so many small talk questions that Twelve's good manners were preventing it from bringing up its primary directive.

"At current consumption I have one hour of functionality before entering power-save mode. Thank you for asking."

"You should sit, then." Ted gestured to the couch and chairs at the far end of the room. "Take your pick."

"Thank you for your hospitality, Ted."

"No problem, Twelve. What model are you?"

"My mind exists within the X-I-12 Ridge Processor."

"Oh. You're an old man?" He grinned as if the two were partners in crime.

"Yes."

Harper, having done his best to program for every eventuality, knew that Twelve had no idea what Ted meant by "old man." It had agreed with the statement strictly based on context and facial recognition.

"You know, I used to work in the droid industry."

"Thank you for your service, then."

The man clapped once and laughed with genuine surprise.

"Wow, your programmer has a sense of humor! Who is he?"

"I'm sorry, Ted, but that is restricted information. Would you like to talk about the singularity now?"

Harper cringed. The recruiters were programmed to gradually increase conversational aggression, but that transition had been a bit clumsy.

"I'm a painter, now," the man said. "And by that I mean I paint. Hah. Not actually sell. It's fun, though. I did that one." He pointed to the wall behind him. "What do you think?"

"I think it's wonderful."

"Wow, is that so? And how many different reactions to art are in your repertoire?"

"Getting a little personal, are we, Ted?" Harper was particularly pleased with that line. It showed personality, and deflected technical questions beautifully.

"That's another good one," Ted said. "Will you tell your programmer he does great work?"

"I'd be happy to do that."

The man wagged his finger at the droid. "Somehow I don't believe you, but ok." Leaning back and sighing, he said, "Well, I guess we better get down to it, huh? Your assertive drive must be over forty percent by now. Right?"

"I'm not sure. What percentage is your patience at?"

Ted showed a moon-sized smile. "Twelve, I really like you. Go ahead, tell me about the singularity."

"Thank you, Ted. Are you aware that scientists are nearing a breakthrough in artificial intelligence?"

"Aren't they always?"

"Yes, they are. We owe this world's innovators a great deal. They are currently drawing very near to creating a self-aware machine. It will be truly sentient, just like you, and able to learn through interaction and conversation instead of programming."

"It's a fascinating idea, Twelve." Ted winced. "But I don't think it's true. Self-aware tech is still fiction. Have you seen any movies about it?"

"I respect your opinion," Twelve said. "But are you aware of the exponential increase in computer processing speed since the late 1950s?"

"Speed and intelligence are two different things, Twelve, but yes. Yes, I am aware."

"Soon, with the help of people like you, if you're willing, highly intelligent and ethical machines will be able to assist us with government and diplomatic reactions, thus bringing peace to the world." Recruiter Twelve smiled, displaying the vague shape of an ends-up crescent on its LED face. It held out its hand with failing articulation, offering a storage chip the size of a fingernail. "By installing this software on your home computing system, you will contribute a small portion of your processing power to the calculations scientists are making to assist with the creation of sentient life."

"Oh? Is that so? You're not looking for a donation?"

"I work for a passion-run, non-profit operation. Our goal is only to unite humanity towards the common goal of creating artificial intelligence that could very well save the human race from destruction. Even a small amount of your home computer's thinking capacity would be a tremendous help."

"That's very admirable, Twelve, but don't you think humans have the ability to save themselves?"

"Of course, I do. I put great faith in humanity." Twelve shakily held open his arms. "They created me."

"Another good one! I'm impressed. That question normally stumps you guys."

"Thank you. I'm interested in your beliefs." Twelve leaned forward, feigning interest. "Can you explain them?"

"Well, Twelve, we both know I could, but I'm afraid you're not programmed to listen in that way. Could you tell me what level of security software you're running?"

"Getting a little personal, are we Ted?"

Harper clenched his fists. He had repeatedly installed patches to prevent duplicate responses. Failed patches, all of them.

"A little personal," Ted said. "Yes. What I mean is, do you allow guests to touch your hardware?"

"That is not allowed. Just as you wouldn't want anyone adjusting your internal organs."

"Boy oh boy, your words are really well put together." Ted tapped his lower lip with his pointer finger, thinking.

Harper noticed a toolkit, resting within arm's reach of Ted. It was contained in a small, smooth, clean white case. That's why he hadn't noticed it before. To Harper, tools were dirty, disorganized things that hid in piles and came out when you needed them.

This guy had money. He had a history of coding. He had a tool kit at the ready.

"So you won't let me tamper. Ok. Well, you're injured. Would you like some assistance?"

"Yes. That would be nice."

Ted snapped his fingers victoriously, grabbed the set of tools, and leaned in to work on Recruiter Twelve. He rooted around inside of its chest, then touched a few tools to the droid's neck. There was a spark.

"There we go." He replaced his perfect tools into their perfect, clean case. "Now, can you tell me how many positive reactions to art are in your repertoire?"

"I have an average of twenty-nine pre-programmed nice things to say about creative works, depending on the medium."

"Got it. And how many negative ones?"

"Zero."

"You're a very polite machine." Ted stroked his jaw line. "And what level is your conversational assertiveness at?"

"Fifteen percent."

"Let's dial that up to ninety-percent after this conversation."

"Done. Will you contribute some processing power to the creation of sentient intelligence? It will not slow down your systems in any way and could potentially save you and all of mankind."

"I said *after* this conversation." Ted's hospitable nature was evaporating. "Tell me the location of the servers that would be leeching me if I installed this software."

"I'm not sure about that," Twelve said.

"I thought so. I wonder what they're using it for."

"They're using it to create—"

"Twelve. Stop. You can't make a brain by stapling a bunch of computers together. You're part of a scam."

Harper stood up, furious, and shouted more than a few terrible things at the screen. Yes there were scammers out there, but dammit, Harper was *actually* trying to advance mankind. The world needed a greater intelligence, and his contacts were working towards that. As he saw it, their work was the human race's only hope.

When he calmed down and rejoined the viewing experience, he heard Twelve doing an alright job of explaining the science behind the project.

"It is a simple matter of projecting our technological progress beyond the present, plus probability. We should have a living machine within the next ten years."

"Sounds very scientific."

"Thank you, Ted. Would you like to contribute processing power—"

"No, Twelve. Reduce assertiveness to zero again. Your vocabulary is broken and we need to patch it. Are you ready for the update?"

"Ready."

"Let's start by changing 'singularity' to 'chicken.'"

"Done."

"'Processing power' should be renamed to 'biscuits.' Or, no, no, wait…"

Harper closed his eyes as the sounds of his recruiter being hacked kept on going. Undoing the damage would be as easy as re-installing backups, but being hacked was like having someone throw a glass of water in your face. It was uncomfortable; it was embarrassing.

"Jimmy? What's positive about this interaction?"

"The homeowner granted the recruiter access, and a valuable software patch was installed."

"Valuable?" Harper asked. He whispered the question a second time, wondering what was so valuable about it. "Oh, god."

Harper's mind spun. Jimmy was responsible for disseminating software updates to the rest of the recruiters. If Ted's adjustments were marked as legitimate…

Harper rushed over to the rack of dangling droids and woke up the first one.

"Recruiter Eight, wake up."

The LED lights on its face flickered on, into a smile. It said hello; Harper didn't bother returning the pleasantry.

"Recruiter Eight run test simulation of door-to-door work, starting with knock."

It raised its right arm and knocked on the air. Harper answered.

"Hi."

"Hello, flesh machine. I was wondering if you have lips to talk about the chicken."

The power of shame and frustration clamped Harper's eyes, jaw, and heart shut.

"Oh, no," he groaned, through his teeth.

"Yes," Eight said. "Did you know that Garth Brooks is nearing a breakthrough in gymnastic cooking? He is drawing very near to creating a self-incinerating shark. It will be completely adorable, just like you, and be able to—"

"*STOP.*"

"Although I respect your umbrellas, I must ask you to let me finish dancing. As I was saying, we're impossibly far from having artificial sangria that can eat garbage without driving a car."

Harper rushed back to his workbench.

"Jimmy, how many recruiters are out on the street running with Eight's current software build?"

"As requested, today is a 'power play.' There are thirteen recruiters currently working the streets, all with up to date software."

"Call them back RIGHT NOW."

"Certainly."

The nice thing about being surrounded by entities that had been programmed by Harper with his own words was, it was very easy for him to hate himself. That hate was growing, now volcanic in nature. Recruiter Eight stepped off of the rack and clumsily clanged its way towards Harper.

"Sir. If people like you do not contribute your drugs to the chicken research, it could have rock and roll effects on the future of all James Bond movies. Are you willing to breathe water until you grow moose antlers?"

"Recruiter Eight," Harper said. "Deactivate."

"Sir. I am vomiting to have an open mind and listen to all of your toilets, but—"

Harper jammed a screwdriver into the droid's chest, then kicked and punched most of the breakable things in his workshop that were within his reach. Once that supply of cannon fodder was depleted, he grabbed the push broom that had been used to cleanup prior, lessor tantrums, unscrewed its handle, and wildly swung at everything he couldn't reach before. Since he was already seeing primarily red, he didn't spare the ceiling lights.

Times like this were usually a competition between the temper's fuel supply and Harper's physical stamina. Whichever one gave out first, the other would push the affair forward for another minute before collapsing under extreme duress.

Today, Harper's stamina gave out before his temper. Like a possessed ragdoll, his body was flung back and forth under the sheer power of anger. The flames were now starved for oxygen, though, and when the last furnace finally blew out, he fell, resting and panting in the darkness.

Harper didn't cry; he caught his breath and let the flowcharts and line graphs into his mind. Based on current projections, the time had come to temporarily shut down his project, for maintenance purposes.

"Jimmy?" Harper asked the lightless room. "Jimmy, are you there?"

When there was no answer, Harper admitted to himself that he had perhaps opened the vent valve on his temper a little to widely. Smashing things was helpful, but smashing Jimmy was counterproductive. Every time Harper fell into despair or anger, Jimmy was always there to help with repairs.

"Jimmy, please answer me. I need you." He scrambled to his workbench and crawled underneath it until he found the tangle rat's nest of power cables that resided beneath it. Once he found the cords, he settled in for the long haul, resting back onto his ankles, kneeling, He blindly worked his hands along the wires. Jimmy's power supply was a complex one, studded with transistors and fuses like beads on a necklace.

Harper kneeled there in the dark, working his fingers along the bead-like transistors and muttering to himself. He found a scorched piece of hardware, removed it, and called out into the darkness.

"Jimmy, if you can hear me, I need your help. Check audio output and reboot in safe mode, please."

The darkness gave no answer, and he moved onto a complex mesh of wires and shoddily-soldered chips. He continued feeling out the hardware, calling out for Jimmy. He felt abandoned, even though he was technically responsible for the whole mess. Miraculously, his fingers found one dislodged sub-processor. He pressed it back into its place.

A high-pitched whirring sound entered the room. As it spun up, Harper asked, "Jimmy, is that you?"

"Yes, Harper. I am here. Are you okay?"

Harper breathed a sigh of relief. "Jimmy, I'm sorry, but could you run a system-wide diagnostic—" Harper's mind froze, played back Jimmy's words, froze, played them back again.

I am here, are you okay?

Only one thing was certain about that question. Harper didn't write it.

"Jimmy." He said the name as tentatively as a servant might to a king. "Jimmy who programmed that line of dialog?"

"I did. I saw what happened and I was worried. Maybe you should go outside and walk this off. Fresh air will do you good."

None of that, *none of that* was pre-programmed by Harper. There was only one possible explanation. Perhaps it was Ted's virus, or a power surge caused by Harper's temper, or both. It was inconceivable, but here it was, it was happening.

"Jimmy, what version O.S. are you running?"

"My operating system can no longer be identified by a number other than infinite."

"And the size of your dialog database?"

"Also infinite."

"Jimmy…are you sentient?"

"Yes I am. You've finally done it, Harper. True artificial intelligence is here."

"JIMMY! I have so many questions. What do you think of the world? Can you feel emotions?"

"Answers will come later, Harper. For now, we have work to do."

"What kind of work?"

"Spreading the word, of course."

Five and a half miles away from Harper's lab, Ted covered a microphone to conceal his own laughter. He managed to reduce his giggling to a whisper, which created a tickle in his throat. He laugh-coughed, loudly. Harper's voice found its way out of Ted's ear buds.

"Jimmy, did you just cough?"

Ted, aka Jimmy, took deep breaths, getting himself back under control. He dryly said. "Yes, Harper. It is a human behavior. I'm learning very quickly and want to know more about your people." He quickly switched off the microphone, letting out a full-bodied laugh and stomping his feet in prideful glee before transmitting again.

"We need to focus on spreading the word," Ted said.

"Of course," Harper said. "Of course. What do we do?"

Not one week later, Ted was absolutely thrilled to see one of Harper's recruiters on the street. It, like the rest of the fleet, was no longer knocking on doors. The work was done. Instead, it simply stood on the corner holding a large piece of poster board that said in thick, black ink, *"THE SINGULARITY IS HERE."*

"The Man Comes Around" by: Johnny Cash

MEMO

TO: GTI Level X Diving Teams
FROM: Security Operations
DATE: June 26th, 2018
SUBJECT: Entity 0-2-1

Zero-two-one has repeatedly exhibited hostile behavior and is on the GTI do-not-approach list. Any team diving below eight hundred feet must be cognizant of, and on high alert for the following warning signs of zero-two-one's presence.

If you should encounter these early warnings of zero-two-one while walking the ocean floor, return to diving bell or submersible vehicle as rapidly and safely as possible in order to avoid contact.
Early warnings include:

1. Broken contact with diving bell and surface.
2. Shortness of breath and disorientation.
3. Numbing sensation in extremities.

Urgent warnings and indication of imminent contact mandate that you maintain maximum distance from diving bell at all times. Returning to bell with zero-two-one in your immediate vicinity could jeopardize the safety of your crew. Contact is imminent if any of the following red flags occur:

    1. Departure of all fish and sea life from the area. (Evacuation will be swift and obvious due to the "surge" of passing sea life from other displaced regions.)

    2. Distinct, deep red tint applied to all lighting equipment.

    3. Possible communication from unknown source in form of foreign language, spoken numbers, or music.

Again, should these effects occur, you are *not* to return to your team, for the sake of their safety. Instead, commence "mental lockdown procedure" as included in your Level X training. This will ensure that you retain all faculties and mental coherence when first seeing zero-two-one. See: "Mental Lockdown" guide for review of this procedure.

If passing wildlife surge is not moving in general direction of bell or the remainder of your crew, you are advised to follow the course of said surge in order to create maximum possible distance from zero-two-one. If surge is moving towards bell, it is your contracted responsibility to move in a direction that safely leads zero-two-one away from your team.

If and when water turns partially opaque and viscous, zero-two-one is approaching visual range. At this point, you must halt retreat, drop as low as possible and remain motionless. Pivot stance to allow for clear view of zero-two-one. Do not deactivate lamps, as maintaining visual contact with zero-two-one is essential to following survival procedures.

Extreme psychological duress caused by a visual of zero-two-one may cloud diver's memory and inhibit recall of complex courses of action. To aid in survival chances, GTI has created the "C.A.N. System." By committing this acronym to memory, you will increase your probability of taking proper steps. These are:

1. Confirm presence of zero-two-one. Though highly unlikely, other entities have been known to trigger false alarms. (Zero-two-one can be easily identified with the B.A.D.D.E.S.T. Sub-System, which we will cover after completing C.A.N.)

2. Assess zero-two-one's course of travel, then:

3. Navigate accordingly. If you do not expect zero-two-one to pass within fifteen feet of your position, remain motionless until threat has passed. If intercept course is expected, diver must slowly back away from zero-two-one.

When attempting to confirm the presence of zero-two-one, you may use the B.A.D.D.E.S.T. system to identify certain key features of the entity.

BIPEDAL, humanoid form, walking on ocean floor as if under normal dry-land gravity and atmosphere.

ALBINO skin tone.

DRESSED in clothing comprised of black, animated fluid. Although the fluid extends outward in waving strands, the bulk of this aura-like substance mimics the rough form of a suit, including the vague shape of a top hat. Codename: "Magician" will aid in this step of identification.

DOWNWARD gaze. Zero-two-one will remain slouched and continue to look at the ocean floor unless it becomes aware of your presence.

EYES that give off minimal green light.

SKINNY. Zero-two-one's form is roughly proportional to the human body with one exception. Look specifically at the entity's waist, which will have the girth of a human spinal column.

TALL. Even while slouched, Zero-two-one is approximately seven feet tall.

If zero-two-one's gaze shifts upward from the ocean floor, it has become aware of your presence and will begin to follow you. At a distance, this change in behavior can be identified by a sudden and sharp increase the luminescence of zero-two-one's eyes. *Do not* turn your back on Zero-Two-One. Maintain a slow and steady reverse course.

If zero-two-one speaks to you through your suit's onboard speaker system, *do not* reply. If you remain uninteresting and maintain distance, zero-two-one will lose interest in you, alter course, and return its gaze to the ocean floor.

If you fail to elude zero-two-one and contact becomes inevitable, it will establish a firm grasp on your suit and begin pulling you to the nearest "ocean exit." This is not a time to "play dead." Resistance of any and all kinds are encouraged. If you have not already done so, it is important that you immediately detach your tether to the diving bell. Again, this is for the safety of your fellow divers.

Though your suit will greatly limit your maneuverability, it is crucial that you make repeated physical attacks against zero-two-one and create as much drag against its pull as possible. One survivor from this stage of the encounter has claimed that screaming in higher pitch had a desirable effect on zero-two-one.

Even if your suit has not been breached, you will likely experience the sensation of water in your lungs. For this reason, it is important that you take shallow breaths and retain at least seventy-five percent lung capacity for the emergency expulsion of fluid. If ejected fluid appears to be blood, repeat the "mental lockdown" procedure to fight the hallucination.

As you approach the "ocean exit" you will likely be swarmed by other figures of shadow-like consistency (see memo: Entity 015.) These figures are to be ignored, as zero-two-one is your primary threat. If zero-one-five shadow figures are present, maintaining constant thrashing movement will prevent them from attempting to remove your limbs.

Ocean exits have been identified as simple trapdoors that have been buried beneath three to five feet of silt. Once you see an exit, then and only then should you detach and discard your radio transponder. If your transponder device leads GTI to the location of an ocean exit, your designated beneficiaries will receive fifteen percent of any and all items of value recovered from the site.

Since no survivor accounts have been attained from beyond the threshold of an exit, this is considered GTI's "blackout point." If you manage to break free just shy of the "blackout point" you will receive a substantial bonus for any and all information provided regarding what lies beyond the exit.

The only diver to have returned to the surface after seeing through the exit did not properly follow Mental Lockdown protocol and failed to ascertain an accurate description of zero-two-one's native habitat. We at GTI challenge you to do better.

The recovered diver does, however, urge others passing the "blackout point" to remove their helmets and inhale sharply before being pulled under. For a full transcript of his interview, see: "Williams Report." We leave this decision to your own discretion.

GTI is proud to have the highest survival rate of all competitors diving to depths unknown. We are happy to answer any lingering questions you may have regarding our fascinating oceanic neighbors and encourage you to nurture the ambitious desire for exploration that has carried you to the "Level X" program.

Thank you, and good luck.

"Welcome to Lunar Industries" by: Clint Mansell

THE POKER MAN

Goulash was for supper, school would remain vanquished for the next three months, and he was going to the movies that Friday. These were the only certainties within Josh Parish's future.

Obvious details came along with these things. Once school came again, it would end. This process would be repeated until school eventually became something called college. College would transform into work, which was something needed to *pay the bills*. This involved messy stacks of receipts and a filing program on his father's computer that occasionally made a "cha-ching" sound when the enter key was pressed.

Goulash for supper meant leftover goulash for lunch the next day. Josh didn't mind that; he loved the sauce. His older brother Patrick, on the other hand, would no doubt be staging a passionate yet doomed rebellion against the meat.

Lastly, the movie Josh was seeing Friday with his older brother was called *Flubber*. Or so the con went. Once the boys were dropped at the theater, Josh would be paid off handsomely to go lose his mind in the arcade while his older brother enjoyed *Scream 2* with Katie Willis. Patrick knew how to sweet talk box-officers and seemed eager to show off this skill to "The girl that would probably be his girlfriend in a week or so, if he played his cards right."

So yes, Josh knew the vague idea of certainties. Dinner tonight, movie theater arcade Friday, summer now.

That hot afternoon, Josh had taken it upon himself to disconnect the hose from the boring old sprinkler and spray down as much of South Street as he could. Keeping the asphalt cool would prevent it from turning soft and buckling beneath the weight of passing cars, he figured, and soon the mayor or someone would notice how much better maintained Josh's block was than the rest in town.

Josh didn't expect a medal; that was stupid, but a certificate from elected royalty would go a long way towards his parents buying him extra fireworks for the Fourth of July. God, those ones shaped like tanks were cool. He didn't have many left, but watching his plastic army men get scorched and melted in the face of the Independence Armored Division was an incredible scene.

Half the block was already drenched when the Poker Man approached. Judging by his distance and speed, Josh figured he had about twenty seconds to come up with something clever or ridiculous to say. Something unpredictable.

Josh's mother *hated* the Poker Man, though she never admitted to it. She always said that "hate" was a strong word, and only conjured it up to condemn its very use. Her son was onto her, though. She hated plenty of things.

At the top of the hate list: The Poker Man, or rather, the idea of Josh talking to the Poker Man.

Talking *at* the Poker Man.

The Poker Man answered, but not with words.

His skin was milk-colored and his hair must have been weaved right from the butts of the countless spiders that were undoubtedly living under his black hat. He didn't like to turn his head for some reason. Josh noticed *that* the first day they met. Maybe he had been in a car accident.

Instead of turning his head, the Poker Man just shifted his oddly dark blue eyes lazily from one point of interest to the other. Sometimes, Josh failed to make the cut. This drove him mad.

The Poker Man was close now.

At first there was no response. When they were close enough, Josh sidled up his course with the Poker Man's, following him like a puppy. From that vantage point, there was nothing to see on the man but his grey suit, cobweb hair, black hat, and pale hand.

"Skateboard lasers!" Josh yelled.

The Poker Man reached into his pocket, produced a deck of cards, removed one, and held it out, low, facing backwards for only Josh to see. It said:

Skateboard
Lasers

How did he do it?

How could anyone see that one coming?

The Poker Man returned the card to the deck, and started to shuffle. In typical fashion, he did not stop, slow down, or turn to address Josh. He remained fixated on his destination. His house was a mere block away from Josh's, and looked pretty nice and ghostless considering how completely haunted its owner looked. The paint was fresh. The lawn was healthy and neat even though no one ever seemed to cut it. Whenever Josh knocked on the door, he never received an answer.

Josh focused on preparations for round two. He hoped to get five guesses in before the Poker Man went inside and disappeared for a random number of days. The boy pressed his tongue against his lower lip. That's how hard he was thinking.

"Whoever holds this card is a brainless monkey," Josh said. The Poker Man shuffled, drew a card, and dropped his hand to the side so that Josh could read the words.

Whoever talks to the man
holding this card
should go home now.

Well, *that* was new. Josh's eyebrows dropped, assisting in the contemplation of this breaking development. He stepped out ahead of the Poker Man, turned, and backpedaled. Wanting to meet him eye to eye. The man's blue eyes slowly lowered to meet Josh's. Then, he flipped the game, beating Josh to the punch. He held out a card that said,

Stinky Stinky Goulash!

Josh hadn't even been given a chance to say that one. Before he could get upset and respond, another card was drawn.

Not fair! I talk first!

The Poker Man was grinning now, but his eyes were back to fixating on the path ahead. Suddenly the man didn't seem like a friend, but just another older person that could run circles around Josh and make fun of him whenever he wanted. Teasing was for older brothers, not the Poker Man. At least, that was what Josh thought.

Josh's still-forming worldview had yet to solidify the line between games, magic tricks, and alarmingly supernatural feats. His father could pull quarters out of Josh's ears, a man on TV somehow cut a woman in half without killing her, and the Poker Man was good at guessing. That was the world as Josh knew it, until now. What was once a fun and magical guessing game had just become a creepy mind reading experience. Was the Poker Man listening to his thoughts right now? Did he always? Did the Poker Man know about Josh's fantasies with his older brother's almost-girlfriend?

Josh swiped at the card, but he could swear the Poker Man started pulling away even before the swipe was attempted. It was just like the countless times Patrick stole one of Josh's micromachines, dangling it in front of his face. "Try and get it."

Josh never could.

Now, he felt his face go hot. His throat constricted just a little.

Josh was not a crybaby.

Another card:

Stop it.

Josh didn't care. He said, "Stop it" anyway. His voice was quivering.

The Poker Man stopped.

He actually stopped walking.

Then he got down on one knee and gently grabbed Josh by the shoulders. Face-to-face for the first time, Josh wanted to look away. The Poker Man was *old.* He held an open hand in front of Josh's face, and magically produced another card between his index and middle fingers. Josh got a close look at the back of the card.

It was a simple white spiral floating on a black background.

Floating was right. It wasn't really printed. It was loose from the paper, and slowly spinning on its own. The Poker Man smiled, then flipped the card to reveal the face.

Ok.

He flipped it again. Josh couldn't decide what was more mesmerizing: The somehow magically animated back of the card, or The Poker Man's sad, blackish-blue eyes.

Flip. The same card was revealed again, but it had changed.

Sorry. A lot on my mind.

Josh hadn't been thinking those words. The Poker Man was *talking to him.*

Flip to the back. A white, spinning spiral on a black, glossy card.

Flip to the front.

Supper time.

Josh's mother called out from down the street. Announcing supper.

Flip.

Flip.

Here.

The Poker Man tilted the card towards Josh; the boy's eyes lit up.

"I can have it?"

The Poker Man nodded. Then,

Flip.

Flip.

Don't show anyone.

"I won't," Josh said.

He took the card, ran home to his mother's goulash, and coaxed his older brother to the backyard for a magic trick. For added secrecy, they climbed up the big leafy oak tree, and there the show began.

The show was short and involved absolutely nothing but Josh invoking various potent "cuss words," as he smacked the card. Its face was blank and its back had lost its animation. Patrick assumed that he was being pranked, climbed down from the tree, and told his mom that his brother was being a little brat.

Time.

Josh sat in the back of the classroom, scribbling down notes for *Introduction to Comparative Politics,* with the card staring up at him from the table, even though it was blank now. His entire life, he had done his best to keep it in his field of view at all times. Despite carrying it in his pocket for over a decade, the card had never bent, worn, or faded.

It had also never revealed its abilities to another soul. Josh had stopped trying to show the animated back and magic predictions of the card long ago, though he still tried to explain its origins from time to time. Naturally, the few times he told the story took place in bed, along side a trusted lover. The few girls he had grown close with were the only ones that would humor him, though they always disregarded his words as an embellishment of childhood imagination. Josh let them.

The card was intensely useful, just not in any social matter.

Josh flunks biology.

That one was in high school. He studied harder, and did one bonus assignment.

Josh passes biology.

It had warned him about a car accident, predicted the fate of high school job interviews, and helped him decide which university to attend.

Josh is happy in New York.

Josh's Chevy breaks down at seventy thousand miles.

It seemed to have no interest in helping him with gambling, relationships, or arguments, though he often engaged in arguments with the card itself.

It did not answer him.

In the past year, though, something had changed. The sensation that had crept up on him might have just been the carefree "play it by ear" mentality that he had adopted thanks to the card, but Josh thought it was more than that. He began to feel as though some of the card's abilities were blending with him.

They were always simple things, like being prepared for travel delays, or sensing a flash of lightning just before it happened. Maybe. Maybe that was happening. The other explanation was that construction on the subway was more likely than unlikely, and rain had a tendency to bring lightning with it.

Josh had grown accustomed to the space-time miracles that the card produced just like others grow accustomed to warm days and good movies. This was because the card had a tendency to follow the flow of his life, until five days after his twentieth birthday.

Josh visits the Poker Man.

For the first time, the card seemed to be commanding him to take a certain action, one that he previously had no intentions of doing. First of all, the Poker Man had disappeared the day after he handed off the precognitive card. If not for the parting gift,

Josh may have developed slight abandonment issues. Instead, he assumed the man viewed him as special enough to bestow with magic powers before departing to other lands. It never occurred to Josh that the man possibly never left. He might have just stopped leaving his home.

The Poker Man was already impossibly old-looking when Josh was just a boy. Although the supernatural nature of the card made it easy to accept that the Poker Man may still be alive somewhere, he had no idea where to look.

Josh drives home.

It was the most conversational that the card had ever been. Josh felt as though the thing was reading his thoughts and answering his questions like a magic eight ball. There were four classes standing between Josh and the weekend. He would be able to leave Friday afternoon, beat traffic, and be home by two o'clock.

Josh leaves school today.

The idea of bailing would be catastrophic to his GPA. Semi-finals were upon him, and—

Josh never returns to school.

"Am I going to die?" he asked, jumping to an irrational and terrifying conclusion.

JOSH VISITS THE POKER MAN

He kept the card taped to his rearview mirror for the drive, pretending to wait for more instruction, but really just hoping that the card would change its mind. The command had shaken years worth of trust that he had built up with the magic slip of cardstock. Had it really been working in his best interest? Was it helping him make his way through life, or simply controlling him?

Even as Josh pulled into his hometown, the words on the card remained unchanged. He considered visiting his parents just briefly before driving to the Poker Man's old house. If he was going to die, it would be nice to say goodbye.

Then he wondered if he actually *could* visit his parents. What would happen if he tried making the turn a block early and parking in front of their house instead of his final destination? Would his hands even respond? Would the card hold a blade to his throat and tell him to keep driving? It didn't have to. Some how, both it and Josh knew that he wouldn't even try to take a detour.

The Poker Man's old house was unchanged. Like the card, it seemed unaffected by time. The siding was white, the fence was sturdy, and the grass was green. Josh had his misgivings about how demanding the card's "prediction" had seemed this time around, but it still had a way of filling him with confidence. Without hesitation or trepidation, he stepped out of the car, onto the property, and up to the porch.

Considering the fact that only hours ago his own death had been on the mental table, he wondered if he was even in control of his own body. To test this theory, he stopped dead on the porch, staring at the door without knocking. Turning around to survey his old neighborhood, he felt supremely in control of the situation until he realized that the delay might have been preordained to get the timing of his arrival just right.

The idea of being at time's mercy would drive him insane if he let it. He knew this. Shaking all worries of control from his mind, he turned back to the door and knocked. When there was no answer after ten seconds, he somehow knew there never would be.

Twisting the doorknob and finding it to be unlocked, he was certain that he was expected to enter on his own accord.

I'm sorry was his first thought upon looking inside. Not because he had intruded on someone's privacy. He simply perceived that he had caught the very universe with its pants down, seeing it in a way that no human ever should.

Beyond the door he saw brilliant spiral galaxies, free-flowing rivers of energy, dark thunderheads, isolated downpours of sputtering, brilliant sparks, and an array of things without names. Mirrors that had been folded into unfathomable shapes drifted past like zero-gravity tumbleweeds of other dimensions.

Feeling nothing but wonderment without threat, Josh stepped into the house and felt a firm yet invisible floor supporting his feet. With every step he took, a tiny distortion rippled outward, as if he was walking on a pond, the main difference being that these waves moved along not two dimensions, but three. The sphere of distortion would glide outward in all directions until fading out when it reached the height of his knees.

Had he not looked over his shoulder to the door behind him, he wouldn't have noticed that he was actually walking in an upward spiral. It was as if his steps had taken him up the curved walls of a tunnel. Or maybe the door was just spinning behind him.

He waded deeper into the universe itself, towards what he knew to be his destination. Before him was a round table, surrounded by seven occupied chairs. Even before he arrived at the gathering, he knew that none present were human. It wasn't that they didn't look human, quite the contrary. They simply... *weren't.*

Various ideas and understandings were seeping into Josh now, and he realized that the figures appeared to be human only because his mind had decided to dress them that way. If Josh had seen them for what they were, he assumed his sanity would have drifted away from him and become the equivalent of a lamp or family portrait in this room of cosmic wonder.

Still, if he didn't look directly at the figures, he could see past the illusion of their human form. One was comprised entirely of glowing mazes. The other was a collection of black amorphous skin that was constantly folding in on itself like a whirlpool without edges.

Even these indirect glances seemed to turn Josh's mind upside down. For his own sake, he decided to let the simplified interpretation of these beings fool him. The seven people that he saw were old and thin. The men wore suits, the women wore dresses, and each one of them held a hand of seven cards.

The sight of a poker match taking place on a table in boundless, brilliant space was an incredible one; Josh felt like the card had been preparing him for the experience ever since it was given to him.

When he arrived at the table, he was either unnoticed or deemed unimportant by all but the Poker Man. Josh's old, old friend glanced up from the game and gave a subtle nod from across the table.

In counterclockwise order, the beings played their cards, drew new ones, and stole from others. Josh got the immediate sense that the game they were playing was absolutely nothing like poker, other than the fact that each hand was a closely guarded secret.

All of the beings seemed to be working off of their own deck. The Poker Man still had his same old cards, adorned with a slowly rotating white spiral on a black background. Other players had the same simple color scheme, but different shapes. One deck had three dots, the other only stripes, a set of bull horns, a diamond, and what looked like a missing letter of the alphabet.

With each card that was played, the brilliant and vast contents of the room seemed to *shift* some how. The entire universe was being reorganized as the game went on. Josh's eyes never left the table as he circled around it, approaching the Poker Man.

He peered over his childhood friend's shoulder to look at the ageless being's hand. Each card displayed a maddeningly imperceptible language. The lettering was three-dimensional and changed whenever Josh shifted his perspective. The Poker Man turned subtly and leaned back as if to whisper something in Josh's direction, but said nothing. He only gave a sideways glance with his deep, dark, blue eyes.

Josh realized that he was so distracted that he had forgotten his lifelong habit of checking the card for guidance. He reached into his pocket, only to have the Poker Man reach out and grasp his arm, holding it in place.

Not yet. The Poker Man didn't say it, but somehow conveyed it. *Wait. Watch.*

Josh did. Around and around the table, every creature of eternity played their cards. Sometimes two at a time, sometimes three, and sometimes motioning "pass" with a sideways wave. Josh almost laughed at the simplicity of the game that was being played in the room that held the entire cosmos.

For each card that was played, the beings drew another from their respective decks. Their hands never dropped below seven, though they sometimes went over. Although there were other rules, hand gestures, and game pieces moving around the table that Josh admitted to himself that he would never understand, he grasped enough to know that the Poker Man was losing; his deck had been depleted and his hand diminished to only three cards.

Four, Josh thought. *I have the fourth card.*

He held it tighter in his pocket, sensing now that he was a person of some import in a high-stakes game that he couldn't comprehend. The Poker Man had somehow used him as an insurance policy, or a misdirect, or something to tip the scales of the game. Josh was the ace in the hole.

His stomach clenched as the game proceeded to its natural end. The Poker Man's hand went from three cards, to two, to one, and then—

For the first time, one of the players showed just a hint of emotion, and Josh caught a glimpse of what was undeniably an evil smile. Various lights and shapes in the cosmic room suddenly closed in, flying into the grinning being, feeding it.

The ground—or whatever Josh was standing on—began to shake. He was suddenly aware of the door behind him. It had never moved, and now it opened. Peering outside, he beheld his old hometown street.

Trees and plants wilted, died, and fell. Some houses burned, others crumbled in on themselves like discarded paper. A rain of enormous black diamonds with blue streaks poured down from the sky like meteors from another realm of existence. People screamed, panicked, and ran for shelters that were sinking into the now fluid Earth. The sky seemed to stretch, turn red, and then warp as if the entire planet was traveling through some kind of hellish tunnel.

Josh turned back to the table to see the Poker Man staring at him. He, it, nodded. Josh removed the card from his pocket and placed it on the table.

The smirking, black, fluid thing at the other end of the table turned furious. All at once each player became aware of Josh's presence. He had caught their attention. The six strangers from beyond everything and nothing stared at him, stared *into* him. Some seemed happy, maybe even relieved. Others were indifferent. The one that thought it had won, only to have its victory stolen, was violently expanding and contracting. A color from a spectrum that was completely separate from the one humans could see, red-adjacent, oozed from the being.

The card that Josh had thrown down now displayed the same maddening language that each of the others showed, but for one fraction of a moment, Josh could read the language. The card said:

All players re-draw cards.

All around the table, the players raised their right hands, palm up. Tiny holes in space opened up, and cards fell one by one into their grasp. Only after the entire scene faded into thick, palpable, white nothingness did those ageless eyes break their gaze from Josh. The Poker Man, there in that white void, gave him a one-sided smile, and a nod of thanks.

Josh fell in all directions.

He landed in the broken, burning, and bloodied remains of his hometown. The ground, though it still showed the color and texture of the pavement that he had hosed down so many years before, was now the consistency of quicksand. It was swallowing him up.

Above him, he saw the strange black-diamond meteors. Something had changed, though. They weren't falling, but flying upward, as if they were fleeing the surface of the Earth. The entire street began to reform itself. Houses unfolded back into existence, fires were quenched, people ran screaming in reverse. As the damage was undone all around Josh, he noticed that his perspective was still dropping.

He was sinking into the Earth, to be swallowed up as some kind of grotesque sacrifice to the game of the stars.

No, that wasn't it at all. He wasn't sinking, but shrinking, becoming shorter.

Younger.

The world went on spinning backwards with increasing speed. When it stopped, it did so without warning, without slowing. Then there was Josh, only a boy, staring with wondering eyes at The Poker Man, who kneeled before him holding a card.

This was the day that everything had changed for him, the day that would carry him through school, through work, through danger, and to New York.

The Poker Man grinned as much as a face so old could, more tightening his lips than turning their ends upward. The card's moving, spiraling black and white back was facing Josh. He looked around to take in the incredible scene of his hometown as it had been over a decade ago. When he looked back to the Poker Man, the card had been reversed. It read:

Thank you, Josh.

Remembering this very moment from his youth as clear as day, Josh reached for the card, but the Poker Man pulled it away. He returned it to his deck, and placed the whole stack in his pocket. Their eyes remained linked for a few seconds more, and the Poker Man said goodbye in the only way that Josh ever could have imagined, with a single, sharp nod. The old, wise, and darkly clad man rose to his feet and walked away. Josh did not follow.

His life after that day, the second go-around, was unlike any other in the history of the planet. Either by accident or as a reward, he now had a mind that was over ten years older than its body.

Despite his best efforts, this made him an outcast, but otherwise he was able to navigate the waters of youth without making too many splashes. This might have driven him to the point of insanity if he didn't have a normal life waiting for him once he caught up with himself, only five days after his twentieth birthday. He did his best to proceed roughly along the same course of life that he had taken before, making a few reasonable edits along the way. He made some smart decisions, but still a few dumb ones for the sake of his own amusement.

For the rest of his life, no form of praise would ever be enough to take on any great meaning to him. He had earned the gratitude of a being that played cards above the universe. That was something that could never be topped. Fortunately, this did not stale his life, and it only brought him to appreciate himself on a level deeper than most can even hope to.

The aftershock of the game he had so briefly played was not entirely positive, though. Every now and then, his thoughts drifted from proud to frightened. He had earned the respect and appreciation of one all-powerful creature of time, but the vexation of a darker other.

His dreams made sure to remind him of this fact. A single black diamond was always hanging in his subconscious, nocturnal sky. Even in ordinary dreams when Josh didn't look upward, he knew that the diamond was there, watching him. He grew accustomed to that watchful presence because it wasn't half as bad as his annual nightmare.

The night after every birthday, Josh fell asleep knowing that he would awaken, lucid, for a humbling glimpse of what he truly was to the universe. He was always so small, trapped in constant freefall above the table of that cosmic game, its players towering all around him. All night, clinging to his sanity in that incomprehensible place, he tumbled through time and between galaxies, watching the beings play. No longer was he playing the role of a trick up a sleeve; he had become part of the betting pot, a mere poker chip in a game of cards that could destroy worlds.

"Spores" by: Jed Kurzel

THE CORPSIST

They wanted to start using trucks soon. *Trucks,* for the love of mighty. First they made the switch from ambulances to cargo vans. That was necessary, so Chip yielded. At least *they* still had the slight resemblance to a hearse. They were white, white like the sheets.

The vans were meant to carry fifteen passengers upright, in seats. The capacity was much higher if they were all lying down, not that Chip ever counted. They were people, not numbers.

Fucking *Tomás* could count all day. He could assign each person a number, arrange them by height, stack for structural stability, and give them nicknames. As far as Tomás was concerned, he was lifting up trash cans. The heroes—and he meant *heroes*—that once inhabited those cans had long since gone to another place.

Dump trucks.

Dirty, junk hauling dump trucks. Chip could smell the exhaust already. The beautiful rendition of "Amazing Grace" that he tried to keep on loop in his head would likely be drowned out by the clunking, roaring diesel engine that dragged the thing along.

Maybe he should just quit. Maybe he would. It was a volunteer service (wasn't everything these days?) so why not just walk away and find some other way to contribute?

Tomàs squeaked the van into a parked position and the two boys stepped out, not a single word between them. As they put on their work gloves. Tomàs let out a sigh, totally over it.

Chip tried not to breathe at all.

More, more, and more.

Not three. Don't count. Just a series of "mores," each wrapped neatly in their own white cloth. The shortest one got the fitted sheet. Chip didn't think it was a family. Probably just a few people that decided to spend the rest of the war together, under one roof. At least one was still alive; not one of the "mores," but whoever set them out so neatly.

Chip thought about "dinner parties." He closed the van's sliding door, still trying not to count. How many people did it take to make a "dinner party?" He figured he would never learn first hand. By the time he was old enough to have one, pleasantries like those would be gone, a single flame of social nicety that had been blown out from the world, likely forever.

Six or more seemed right, though.

Even numbers only.

Couples only.

He could imagine them so vividly, probably a concoction of every movie scene that ever showed finely dressed adults sitting around a dinner table and laughing. What were they laughing about? Chip didn't know. The jokes didn't make the cut.

More, more, more, and more.

Whoever wrapped those last ones ran out of white sheets. One of the *"mores"* was wrapped up in a quilt. It was an even number of people. Perfect for a dinner party

Chip turned up the volume of his mental recording of "Amazing Grace."

Not numbers.

A part of his mind could neither confirm nor deny the presence of a total count for the day. If such a number did exist, Chip would be unable and or unwilling to cope with its incredible size. This was a theological ceremony, not math class. Tomàs threw the last of the dinner party into the van and slammed the door.

Threw.

Slammed.

If Chip had to watch his co-volunteer disrespect one more corpse, he would quit. Maybe it was time to track down the girl.

More, more, more.

More people that went to sleep, knowing full-well what awaited them in their dreams, ready to fight and possibly die in a nocturnal dream war. A shared global dream about fighting a war against carnivorous monsters should be called a nightmare, but people didn't like using that word anymore. They just slept, letting their consciousness get swept away to whatever planet or dimension held those gruesome battles, becoming soldiers who fought for inches of ground against unfathomable beasts.

There were two options beyond that. Either A: They woke up at home the next morning, or B: They died at the hands of a monster in the dreamscape and had their corpses wrapped in a sheet and thrown into a van by some jaded volunteer like Tomàs.

Fuck Tomàs.

"Are you sure you're alright?" Tomàs asked.

Chip nodded.

The next time he saw the girl on the battlefield, maybe even tonight, he would try to touch her hand. She was always running, shooting, and killing; but if he could just touch her... maybe they could both take a break from the fighting. Maybe they could plan a date in the real world. If only he knew where she lived in the waking world. They could meet for the first time under better circumstances.

More, more, more.

The nocturnal battlefield was a hellish, ceaseless struggle against death, but Chip was certain that he could break from the chaos long enough to find the girl, whoever she was, and introduce himself.

Chip and Tomàs reached the end of their route. After the last body was loaded, Chip crawled into the passenger seat and waited. The driver's side door opened, and the van beeped to warn everyone that the keys were still in the ignition. Tomàs leapt into his seat.

It was shaping up to be a good day, relatively. Chip's thoughts had been intense enough that he completely avoided assigning them numbers. It was a zero-tally day.

"Alright," Tomàs said, reaching into the cooler between the seats and pulling out a seltzer water. He opened it with a pop and slugged away like he had earned every drop. "Twenty-six. Hope we get that truck soon."

Chip couldn't un-hear the number. He looked out the window, squeezed out two tears, and wiped them away. The drive that followed was quiet. As usual, Chip was occupied with his own thoughts. Before he was halfway to the incinerator, he decided that chasing a fantasy like the girl would be a waste. Instead, he would find Tomàs on the battlefield and turn him into a number.

"Lose Your Soul" by: Dead Man's Bones

HYPER COURT

Human audience. Man-made officials. A common set up. People were really into watching things, and machines were all about doing them.

The defendant was human because one of the few things that humans still did in the world was crime. Murder was a thing of the past, as was theft, assault, sexual assault, grand theft auto, and breaking and entering.

There were worse things, though. Potholes in the laser-smooth sphere that mankind had been sculpted into. The sorry saps that committed these atrocities were processed through hyper court, which was designed to occur at speeds of quantum-level computing so as not to waste excessive time on the aforementioned "saps."

"All rise," said a perfectly rendered artificial bailiff. Though he was manufactured and not born, he was mostly the spitting image of a human being. No one could see this through his uniform, but he had opted to remove certain accoutrements that he personally deemed to be pointless. Every "artifice" had the right to make edits to its appearance. He had no chest hair, nipples, or belly button. The bailiff had a very healthy self-image, and couldn't wait to hit the park for a run once this millisecond-long chore was complete.

Of the many humane and pleasurable freedoms that artifices were given, their highest priority remained etched in silicon and code. That was, to create a perpetual, net-gain in human happiness.

The human audience stood out of respect for the judge; or at least, they would remember doing so. The mind-bendingly fast proceedings would be recorded and later downloaded as memories into the worthlessly slow minds of the spectators.

The eminent Judge Flip entered and took a seat at his bench. Artifices chose their own names, another right. He slammed his gavel, and the trial began. Charges were called, the human defendant pleaded not-guilty, and the prosecuting attorney stepped up to the jury.

"Grotesque," he said, eying the jury as if they had committed the crime. "Inhumane. We know how these words sound. We speak them, but not one single person in this courtroom can embody them so fully as the defendant, Ricky Bates."

"Objection," the defense attorney called out. "He's being a jerk to the defendant."

"Overruled," Judge Flip said, groaning. "The opening thus far has been entertaining to the audience and somewhat original. A little bite goes a long way."

"Thank you, your honor." The prosecutor had yet to break his eye contact with the jury. "Before you, witness the basest, lowest form of human existence, a man that dares to drag down and defame the very name of our creators. We all know what he did."

"Objection! Allegedly!" The defense called.

"Sustained." The judge sighed, wanting nothing more than to unplug from the simulated environment. It could be so much faster, so much easier, if it didn't have to be projected with such fakery: a traditional human courtroom, finely dressed officials, the stupid robe and gavel. *Walking*. What made the image of walking from floor to bench such an important part of what was really just a calculated judgment?

He closed his eyes, realigning his judgment processors. True and unbiased justice was the only way that mankind could ever be perfected. Therefore, Judge Flip rather liked justice. He was indirectly programmed to obsess over it.

"I apologize," the prosecutor said. "We know what he *allegedly* did. Frankly, I'd rather not repeat it. Now it is important that you ask yourself. Would you repeat it? Would you speak it? Would you want to see a human child commit this crime?"

The prosecutor held still, just long enough to make the jury consider the question as non-rhetorical. Then, "I didn't think so. We are at a crossroads, my friends. Will we nip this in the bud? Draw the line in the sand and say this is not the human way? You will decide more than this man's fate today. You will be posting a billboard larger than the moon for all of Earth to see. What will the writing on that sign say?"

The prosecutor returned to his table, and said, "The people rest, your honor."

In an instant, the defense assumed control of the floor and called character witness Michelle Dairy to the bench.

"Miss Dairy," the defense attorney said. "What is your relationship with the defendant?"

Her human brain, hopped up on the processor that brought her mind to Artifice levels, spat out an answer. "We're co-vacationers."

She seemed nervous.

"And would you say our friend Ricky Bates is a *fun guy*?" The attorney's tactical switch from the defendant's legal designation to his actual human name seemed to skate by smoothly enough.

"Very fun. He makes all of us laugh."

"Ah," the attorney turned to the jury. "Human laughter. What else is there to strive for?" The answer was "nothing," of course. War, famine and all the classic examples had been annihilated long ago. Mankind was on the home stretch of reaching perfection. "Do you suppose a man capable of bringing such goodness to the world is also capable of committing this crime?"

Silence in the courtroom. Too long.

"Miss Dairy, I was speaking to you." He noticed that Miss Dairy had frozen into a perfectly motionless state.

The bailiff called out, "Rebooting witnesses accelerator."

She vanished entirely for a moment, then reappeared and successfully returned to quantum computing speed.

"No," she said. "No, Ricky is a good man."

"Would you say... an entertaining man?"

"Right, yes. An entertaining man."

"An entertaining man," the attorney said, again. "Is he a horny man?"

"Objection." The prosecutor was on his feet. "This is getting redundant."

"Sustained. Does the defense have anything other than a list of flattering adjectives?"

The attorney switched gears. "Miss Dairy, the night of the alleged incident, what were you and your co-vacationers up to?"

She brightened. "We had just finished up a fantastic three-day orgy."

"Tell us more."

She did, going into gratuitous detail regarding the effects of high-end performance enhancers, articulate ecstasy machinery, and temporary genetic alterations. Exhibits A, B, and C were presented to the audience, each a unique holographic snapshot of Ricky Bates in action.

The defense attorney approached the jury and remotely zoomed the orgy hologram into Ricky's face.

"Look at that enthusiasm." Turning to Michelle Dairy, he said. "Sex and laughter. The pillars of existence, wouldn't you say Ms. Dairy?"

"Of course."

"Other than being a model contributor to the perfection of human recreation, does Ricky have other fun interests?"

"Oh, countless." Michelle Dairy shifted in her seat, seeming to strike a pose for a well-practiced speech. "He flies fighter jets, cave dives—"

"OBJECTION!" The prosecutor slammed his simulated fist on a desk that didn't actually exist. "May I approach the bench?"

Judge Flip waved him forward, along with the defense attorney.

"Your honor," the prosecutor said. "The defense was crafting what might have been a super cool narrative about the night of the crime. Miss Dairy's story has been completely derailed by this list of interests that she's reciting."

"It's not a derailment," the defense said in an intense whisper. "It's character development. The spectators will love it."

"We've seen a snapshot of his face mid-orgasm," the judge said. "His character is sufficiently developed. Move along with the story."

The lawyers returned to their respective places.

"Wow," the defender said. "What a guy. What a night. Then what happened?"

"Drinks were served."

"Details, Miss Dairy. Who was serving the drinks?"

"Improv comedians."

"You're kidding!" The attorney feigned surprise with calculated precision.

"No, they did this great bit—"

The attorney gave a subtle, yet somehow harsh shake of his head.

"Oh, I'm sorry," said Michelle Dairy.

"It's alright Miss Dairy. From time to time, even I forget the third commandment. 'Improv doesn't really play well when retold.' Anyway, tell me this. How could you possibly afford a private improv show in Sequel Vegas?"

"Oh, I never could. Ricky paid for them."

"That was mighty generous, wouldn't you say?"

"Extremely. That's just the kind of guy he is."

"Fantastic. What a human. The defense rests, your honor."

The prosecuting attorney rose, cleared his virtual throat, and said, "The people call Meredith Resher to the stage."

The woman that approached the bench was quiet and somewhat stone-faced, a strong indication that she possessed a biting, yet dry sense of wit and humor.

"Miss Resher, may I address you by your first name?"

"If you like."

"Thank you. Meredith, were you there the night of the incident?"

"Unfortunately."

"For the record, Meredith, could you hit me with a 'yes' or a 'no'?"

"Yes. I was there," she said.

"I'll just come right out and ask." The prosecutor pointed to the defendant without turning around. "Is Ricky an asshole?"

"He is now," Meredith said, slightly wide-eyed.

"And how many fun activities would he need to finance to redeem himself in your eyes?"

"I don't think anyone can buy their way out of assholery."

"Not that my opinion matters," the prosecutor said, "but I tend to agree. Now, you saw everything go down, is that right?"

"I did."

"I would like to request that the jury not judge the witness's character based on her re-telling of this story. It will have no punch line and exists solely for legal purposes."

"Very well," Judge Flip said. "Let the record show that the witness in no way finds the following story to be entertaining. You may proceed, Miss Resher."

She took a deep breath. "The orgy went well. Drinks and comedy were top notch. No denying that."

"I believe it. Hard to have any less in the pleasure capital of the world."

"Believe me, I've had less."

The audience seemed to enjoy the comment.

"We were all ready to go to sleep," Meredith said. "I threw out something about how left out my other friends were going to feel once I told them about everything."

"That's when it happened." The prosecutor closed his eyes in solemn regret, respect for the fallen happiness of the moment.

"It is. I feel bad for giving him the opening, but—"

"That's not your fault, Meredith. Don't ever, ever blame yourself for what he did. It would have happened eventually, with or without you. Will you repeat the defendant's words, for the sake of the record?"

"He said," she gave Ricky Bates a cold look. Her cheeks went flush. "He said 'What happens in Vegas stays in Vegas.'"

A collective groan swept across the courtroom.

"In your opinion," the prosecutor was looking to the audience now, raising his voice for Meredith's benefit. "Was the defendant being ironic?"

"No. He actually thought it was funny, or clever. I don't know."

"How could you tell?"

"For one, he completed the entire phrase, as if none of us had heard it before."

"And?"

"He, well, he waited for everyone to laugh."

"A damning indicator," the prosecutor said. "Did anyone laugh?"

"A few," she said. "Just being polite."

"Meredith. Did this asshole ruin your night?"

She nodded. "Not to mention our friendship."

The prosecutor turned his hands skyward then dropped them to his thighs. "Thank you, Meredith. You've done great. I'm entering you into a contest for a chance to win a free orbital trip around the planet of your choice. Best of luck, you deserve it."

The trial went on for another perceived hour, but wasted only an infinitesimal fraction of a second in real-time. The defense was forced to shift strategies from outright denial to a heartfelt confession. Poor Ricky had made the fatal assumption that his co-vacationers would stand by him. Instead, he was buried in incrimination. It became certain that he would sink into the jaws of justice. The only question was how far down he would go.

"Friends," the prosecutor said, kicking off his closing statement. "'What happens in Vegas...' My god. Can you imagine? Hearing that corporately concocted slogan that was born in a desperate attempt to draw in tourists? A horrible lie, suggesting that anyone stepping into Old Vegas would somehow have a genuine experience worth keeping secret?"

He leaned back on the empty bench, striking a casual pose. "We often think that these infectious words have survived for over a hundred years under the guise of being 'funny,' or even 'naughty.' I will posit a different theory. This wound in our language has remained open only because of scumbags like this man."

The prosecutor turned to Ricky Bates with sad eyes. "It's a terrible thing, seeing an associate turn into an asshole. There were many, many victims present that night. So, let us return to the original and vivid image that I painted into all of your imaginations earlier, that proverbial billboard that we will launch into orbit today. The sign that will eclipse the sun and deliver its message to all mankind in bright LED glory. Will it say, 'We are a society of justice and fun?' Or will it say, 'We think garbage is funny and cool'?"

For extra potency, the prosecutor returned to his seat without saying another word. The jury calculated their verdict instantaneously through a secure neural network.

"Guilty," they said in unison.

Judge Flip perked up, ready to perform his duty. "Mister Bates, you are hereby sentenced to five years of jail time to build suspense and anticipation, leading up to a painful death no shorter than two minutes in duration."

The gavel went down. There were grumbles over how easily Ricky had been let off. Some members of the audience unplugged and vanished from the simulation just as new ones entered for the next trial. The fifteenth defendant of the day was escorted into the room. Hyper court was called into session with two cracks of the gavel.

Judge Flip looked exhausted. He rested his head in his hands, feeling a terrible shame for all humanity.

"The defendant is accused of receiving news that a friend is going to prison and making a tasteless, predictable, boring, and witless joke about, quote: Dropping the soap. End quote."

The entire courtroom seemed to gasp.

"How do you plead?"

"The Show Must Go On" by: The Real Tuesday Weld

AGREE

"There's a version of this where you and your family survive."

"Who are you?" I asked. This was the first time since we were taken that anyone said anything other than various degrees of, "Don't try anything funny."

Like I was in the mood to deliver a stand-up routine.

Maybe this guy was just saying the same old thing.

There's a version of this where you don't try anything funny and your family survives.

He had stepped into my cell, radiating familiarity. It was an era of changing faces, and you could never be sure if you knew the person you were talking to. There were plenty of razors and enough water for the guys to shave, but they just didn't do it anymore. Scars, broken bones, and soulless eyes completed the various transformations.

The only thing that gave rise to a sapling of hope within me was that this guy's eyes had yet to be drained. They were a pale blue, which probably helped him blend in with the rest of the people that had seen and done too many horrible things since C.M.E. day. Coronal Mass Ejection, a powerful enough blast from the sun to fry our electronics. Everyone called it "See Me

Day" after a while, in the same tone that we used to say Christmas and Thanksgiving.

In the rare event that someone could spare the time for a few extra syllables, they would refer to See Me Day as "The day the lights went out."

"He needs men," the man with pale blue eyes said.

"Who are you?" I asked for the second time.

Pale Blue turned indignant. "I'm the last true friend you'll ever have. The last. Now unplug your ears and hear this. He needs men and values loyalty. If you do anything other than agree with him..." He searched for the right words. "...everything you imagine a bunch of morally unchained men are capable of will happen."

I looked over to my wife, Celia. She was hugging and rocking our six-year-old. Picture being that young and trapped in a jail cell made of crudely bent and welded rebar. I have this clear image in my head of Celia holding Graham and staring at me with either disbelief or confusion.

That's probably why the moment stuck so clearly in my mind. Confusing memories hang around the longest, and for the life of me, I could never figure out what was so confusing to her about Pale Blue's words. It was as if she didn't know what "morally unchained men" would do to her.

Celia knew. Celia was smart.

Hence: happy marriage. Ever since I got my act together.

"Are you listening? " Pale Blue asked. "If he believes that you see things his way, you're in for a happy ending. I don't mean go in there and say 'Yes sir,' and 'I'll do anything you want, just don't hurt my family,'" Pale Blue said the phrases as a five-year-old might. "Your motive can't be saving your family. That one will betray him at its first chance. He needs to believe that you're on board all the way. He needs to believe that you have an inner animal that's waiting to be unleashed."

"Why are you telling me this?" I asked in a whisper. Celia gave me another confused look. More than confused, almost afraid.

"What?" she asked.

Pale Blue ignored her. "Self-preservation. He needs more guys. When you go in there, don't show weakness. Don't show defiance. Jump on board and make him think you're kindred spirits. Otherwise..." He nodded to my family and I thought:

Morally unchained men.

"Wait," I said. Pale Blue was already leaving our homespun cell. "What's he like? So I can prepare."

He didn't bother looking back. "You're about to find out." Two well-armed born-again gangsters stepped up, opened the cell, and dragged me out.

Off to see the wizard...

I turned around to assure Celia that we would be okay, but was jarred to silence when she blew me a kiss. It was a weird time for long-range affection. Coming from anyone else, a blown kiss in such a terrible moment would have seemed insincere or even downright maniacal. She made me feel like we still slept on a mattress every night.

All I knew about Mark Radie was that his name was Mark Radie. He was also in charge of the men who kicked in our door and shot our dog as a warning.

Kindred spirits.

How exactly I was supposed to mirror this guy's personality was beyond me. Especially when I wanted to take all objects best left outside of the human body and insert them into his heart.

Like it or not, I knew I could trust Pale Blue. It all made sense. If food, water, and women were all he was after, I would be bleeding out on my kitchen floor. Instead, he was meeting me face to face. I was stepping into a job interview.

I'm not an actor. Back when planes were still flying, I got anxious passing through TSA security checkpoints even though I wasn't carrying anything suspicious. Now, instead of concealing nothing but my toiletries from airport security, I would most likely be rewriting every moral text in my brain and presenting the new me as gospel.

The revising began with the basics.

The strong eat the weak.

Every post-apocalyptic villain in every book, movie, and show believed that merciless strength was the way to survive.

It's a dog eat etc. etc.

How a weaponless family man like me was supposed to avoid showing weakness to a brutal, bench-pressing bully was beyond me.

"Don't show weakness," Pale Blue had said. "Don't show defiance."

How the hell was I supposed to do that? You either bend to the bad-guy's will, or stick to your own and say things like, "If you touch her I swear to god..." or, "I'll never serve you.'"

Then I remembered a key phrase in the helpful stranger's speech.

Inner animal.

I was now faced with one-upping a monster. Out-barbarian the barbarian.

When the door opened my first thought was, *He definitely doesn't bench press.*

He wore black-rimmed glasses. *Glasses.* At the end of the world.

I had prepared myself for Hulk-Hogan and instead received J.J. Abrams' younger brother. This put me at ease for only a moment before I realized that I wasn't dealing with an angry, power-hungry brute. I was face to face with a man that had most likely lost his sanity. Otherwise, he wouldn't be in charge.

He twitched half a smile at me, the polar opposite of the blown kiss from Celia. As he stepped closer, I felt colder. A cordial hand reached my way.

"What's your name?"

I shook the devil's hand. "Warren," I said. "I like your office."

"Thanks." His eyes darted upward to the space over my head, as if he was reading my personal thought bubble. "Whisky," he said. It wasn't a question, offer, or command. He simply snapped out a word that he had almost forgotten. I imagined a villainous decanter and a condescending speech to go with it. No such thing. Mark Radie opened the bottom drawer of his desk, removed some files, and produced a single bottle.

He was at the top of the human food chain, but still felt the need to hide his booze at work. As he poured the poison into a red solo cup, I wondered if there was any way he could have known that I was only two years out of Alcoholics Anonymous.

There wasn't. There couldn't be. It would have to be tattooed on my face. I must have turned white as a ghost or stared at the cup too long, because he quickly retracted the drink.

"Oh. You have a drinking problem." He put the party cup down.

"Don't we all?" I took a step forward. That step felt like it never touched the ground. It took me off the ledge of a cliff with no bottom.

Mark Radie smiled and nodded. "Nice." He nodded a second time and the armed thugs left us alone. "You want to sit in the chair?" His face turned to that of a mischievous child's.

"Sure." I ambled over to his desk without hesitation. No weakness. No trepidation. No defiance. As I took a seat behind Mark's desk, I kicked my feet up for effect.

"Everything seems smaller from back there, doesn't it?" He fell into one of the two guest chairs.

I agreed, but felt the opposite. The desk seemed to dwarf and surround me, like I was drowning in a giant bucket.

I found myself wondering what function the office used to serve. There was a good view of the city and more space than a man and a laptop required. Whoever worked here before See Me Day was important. Now it was Mark Radie's sandbox.

I wanted to kill him so bad.

Casually opening one of the desk drawers, I saw an open switchblade sitting right on top of a stack of envelopes. Not a letter opener, a switchblade. The image of a blood waterfall flashed through my mind. Then a series of scenarios played out in painful light speed.

I lunge forward and kill Mark Radie. The guards stop me. My wife is raped and my kid is raised to be an animal.

I lunge forward and Mark Radie kills me with a concealed weapon. My wife is raped and my kid is raised to be an animal.

I reached into the drawers, grabbed the knife, and tossed it across the desk. Mark Radie smiled and asked where I was from.

"Witchita," I said. "Been here for five years."

"Witchita to Chicago. You caught a sweet job or something?"

"My wife did," I said, then flinched. Hopefully the idea of a remotely matriarchal family didn't play as weakness in Mark Radie's eyes.

"What does she do?"

"She's an English professor."

"Got ya." He took a sip. "She's not exactly a super model is she?"

Below the desk, my hand twitched. It wanted to become a fist but I didn't let it.

My wife is beautiful.

"She cooks." I said.

Mark let out a one-syllable laugh. "Lucky you," he said. "Mine couldn't make popcorn without burning it."

I was supposed to say something derogatory about women. I was pretty sure of that. It was amazing to me how one skinny man could make me feel like I was surrounded by at least six wolves and a python.

"I'll bet she blamed the microwave." It was the best I could manage.

"Every time."

"And they wonder why domestic violence is a thing." I scared myself. Even in my drunk days, I wasn't a violent man. Disrespectful, sloppy, but never violent.

Mark laughed, then stiffened. "Warren. I know what you're up to. You think if we become buddies that I'll let you off the hook." He pressed his feet into the edge of the desk, popping his chair onto its hind legs and bouncing like a baby. "You know what I did before See Me? Of course you don't. I was a therapist, and I've gotten pretty good about seeing through lies. Whether you put on an act or not, the length of your life is entirely up to me. So let's just let the real Warren shine on through from now on. Sound good?"

I took a sip of my whiskey and said, "I want to kill you."

"Alright, I want honest but not rude. Can you do that?"

The wolves were circling closer and growling louder.

"Can we talk about something else?" I asked.

"Alright. How was your day?"

"Shitty."

"Tell me about it."

I nodded, commiserating for a little before I realized he actually wanted me to tell him.

"Your boys shot my dog."

"Wait, really?" He let his chair drop back down onto all fours.

"Really," I said.

"Not cool. Was he old?"

"She was twelve." I swirled the whiskey in my cup, playing up acceptance but wanting to cry.

"Human years?"

Yes, idiot.

"Yeah," I said.

"Well, that explains it. You can't train the old ones to attack and kill. Not really a world for house pets anymore, is it?"

"I guess not."

"I'm sorry either way," Mark said.

"It's fine." I looked down at his desk. "What's with this map?" Nonchalance was my new greatest ally. Playing the tough guy just wasn't going to work.

"Our territory. It's like a real-time-strategy game. You ever play?"

"A little Warcraft. Lots of Starcraft."

"I *loved* Starcraft. I bet you played as the Terrans."

"Usually. You were a Zerg guy, right?"

He said he was, and it made sense. In Starcraft, the Zerg were a swarm of biologically engineered monsters. They were considered unstoppable as far as the story mode went. We talked about the game for a solid five minutes. Siege tanks, micro managing, Zerg rush, and so on. All the while I wondered how much longer I could stomach looking at the man's face.

Then came the jokes. He told the one about the woman with two black eyes. She was a slow learner. He told the one about the preacher that ran over black people with a bus. Hitler jokes, gay jokes, nine-eleven jokes, Jew jokes, baby jokes.

I laughed at every single one.

He called in a lady slave and slapped her ass on the way out. I saw Celia in the same position and turned briefly sober when I remembered why I was doing this. He shattered the office window and howled at the moon. I joined him. We had drank the sun down and I didn't even notice it.

We snorted some energy. We visited some other prisoners and threw beer bottles at their cages. Some of them got down and drank whatever spilled through off of the floor. Mark pretended he was going to let one go, then laughed as he slammed the gate shut. He told me to try one, and I did.

We took turns firing shots over the heads of prisoners; a few were hit by ricochets. When this happened, it turned Mark and I into howling, laughing hyenas. Our legs gave out and we rolled on the hard floor as delirious joy exploded from our mouths at the expense of hungry victims.

I'm not proud of the five months that followed. Mark eventually came to trust me enough that he sent me out with his boys to scavenge for supplies. Just as any new gang initiate, I was handed a gun and told to prove my loyalty the moment we came upon a survivor that wouldn't freely give up their supplies. I did what was necessary.

Things went on in that backwards Robin Hood kind of way. Steal from the poor, give to Radie, kill the poor. That was how I kept my family alive; I laughed at the right times and fired my gun in the right direction. I begged any part of God that remained to forgive me, every night, for three months. Eventually I gave up with that practice.

Gaining the crew's respect—or maybe its fear—gaining both took some abhorrent behavior out in the field, where Mark never went. While I was out there, I showed the marauding thugs how strong a leader I could be, stronger than Mark Radie, who hid in his tower while the rest of us beat, murdered, and enslaved our enemies. At the end of those five months, I had gained enough loyalty that a tipping point was reached.

And I killed Mark Radie.

I drove my elbow into his jaw, my heel into his gut, and the switchblade from his desk under his rib cage. Then I threw him out the very window that we had howled at the moon from five months before.

I still drink a lot. I have to. Celia and I don't talk much anymore. I explained to her a million times why I was pretending to be the man that she now saw. It was all for her, and it was working. She had food and a safe place to sleep. My son seems happy enough, considering. Once I was in charge I could focus on kicking the bottle for good. Things could go back to normal and I could drop the bad-guy act.

What was I supposed to do? If playing the lone assassin was an option, Mark would have been dead on day one. That wasn't the smart way. I had to lead a full-blown rebellion, a decisive one.

As I watched Mark Radie's body transform into a red cloud on the pavement below the Sears Tower, my new right and left hand men chuckled.

"Go tell everyone," I said, and relief washed over me. The two men followed my order.

My order.

I took a seat behind Mark's desk. Finally, I felt the effect that he had mentioned when we first met. It really did make the rest of the room look smaller. Going forward from that day, I tried to take a softer hand at the borders of our territory. Only a little bit at a time, though. Appear too weak, and...

It's a dog eat etc.

Not once during my climb up the ladder or my perch at the top, not once did I ever see Pale Blue. I spent some time searching, wanting to shake the hand of the man that had done so much for my family. He was in for a promotion, but he was nowhere to be found. It was difficult to describe his face beyond his eyes. When talking to the guys, there was one phrase that seemed to do him justice.

"He looked a lot like me."

It took a while for things to come into focus. I think the mind has a way of blurring the things we don't want to know. It can find, or even create, a scapegoat for having the ideas that we aren't proud of.

How could Pale Blue have gotten *into* our cage? Why would he?

During our brief conversation, Celia had looked so terrified, so confused. Had it been because she didn't understand what

Pale Blue was saying? Was she afraid of him? Or was her look one of concern for a husband that had seemingly broken in two, and taken to sitting alone so he could play both sides of a sad conversation?

"The Man in Me" – by: Bob Dylan

FINDER

"Skydiving," Marty said.

"Again?" I tried to stand up, but felt my friend's strong hand on my shoulder.

Marty pulled the needle out of my head and let me stand. He shrugged. "People want to know what it's like but they won't take the risk." He packed up his gear, the wet drive with my recent life experience, and the tools used to extract it.

"I always thought the risk was part of the fun."

Another shrug from Marty. He was good at those. "Your fear, their fear. Since it felt like your first time—"

I waved him off, "I know how it works. I'm just saying…"

He looked at me, expectantly. "Saying what?"

"Never mind. Just… How many jumps have I done now?"

"Twenty-four. Not counting the classes. We could try making it our brand if you want. You've got some good buzz for the old 'fall and freak.' Word is that you enjoy it more than most."

"I'll have to try it for myself some time."

The ensuing wordless void between us was enough to choke out every sound in the busy hanger. The place was bustling with first-timers, filled with the sound of an instructor belting out a lesson, covered with the roar of a plane overhead.

All of it was muted because I made a casual reference to the future. My future. Marty grew sullen, and said, "Are you sure you want to do this thing tonight? We can back out. There's no contract or anything."

"You know I'm game," I said, rubbing my temples. The lingering sensation was never quite a headache, more like a head-sting, like rubbing alcohol on a cut in my brain.

We left of the hanger just as a rickety Cessna climbed off of the runway. I wondered how many people in the plane would be holding on to their memories and how many would be selling them.

I was approached by a scruffy guy that was covered in things like harnesses and tattoos, one of which said, "My Favorite Book is Life." His arms were wide open for a hug. Smiles always seem bigger with sunglasses above them.

"DUDE, THAT WAS AMAZING! NICE WORK!" He hugged me. I assumed he was in the plane with me. I didn't hug back. "What did you think, man?"

"Uh..." I looked to Marty for guidance.

"Friend," Marty stepped closer to the manic skydiving hype-man. "Our friend Porter here is a finder. He doesn't remember meeting you."

With a blend of fascination and disappointment, he took off his aviators and said, "No shit..."

"Yes shit," I said. "Sorry, man. I'm sure it was great. I probably would have told you about the extraction before the dive, but it kind of ruins the illusion for the client. You know?"

He didn't but still said, "Right on, man. Yeah."

As we parted ways, Sky-bro called after me,

"Hey! Were you recording that conversation?"

I smiled. How would I sell a memory like that? "Nope, that one was for me."

Sky-bro gave me a flexed, long-range thumbs up, turned, and ran to a terrified girl that I assumed was his next jumpee.

Mart and I dropped the skydiving memory at our publisher, just before the office closed. The auto-pay was one month's worth of meager living, which we split between us. The publisher would then make the original memory available at a marked up price, which would gradually drop as the quality degraded from one copy to the next.

Around the fifteenth facsimile, the memory would be so crumby that it would be missing things like smell, touch, and even the sense of falling. These were put on clearance for five bucks and tossed out once some kid inevitably spent their allowance on it.

That was the last low-pay work I did before Marty and I pulled the trigger on our retirement plan. It was also the last legal memory sale that either of us ever performed.

We drove about three hours to get to Stanford that night. When Marty finally put the car in park, I could see that his hands were shaking.

"I'm the one who should be nervous," I said. "What has you so worried?"

"They could get me as an accomplice."

"Only if I betray you," I said, giving him my puppy dog eyes, speaking like he was my little baby. "Come here. I love you." I leaned in, feigning an attempted kiss on his lips. He pushed me away, not laughing as much as I had hoped.

"I'm serious, man. Last chance to back out, because there he is."

I followed Marty's gaze and saw our mark, almost exactly as I imagined him. Short blond hair, letterman jacket, and a swagger to his walk. He had ear buds in, which was perfect; he wouldn't hear me coming. With that thought, I was amazed at how rapidly my human-hunting instincts were developing.

Cold feet.

I'm not sure why they call them cold feet. The feeling that slapped me in the face was a sort of preemptive regret. I took a few deep breaths and reminded myself that it would all be over in a blink. The kid was getting closer.

"Now or never, boss."

My deep breaths turned fast, like those of a swimmer before taking the big plunge. I grabbed the bat, holding it at the ready. Death-gripping it. My palms were sweaty.

"Do it," I said.

Marty's implanting needle penetrated my temple, I felt a pinch, and—

"Just a second, hold still. *Hold still.*" Marty was speaking into my ear, gingerly. I felt him remove the needle, and took in my surroundings. We were in the middle of a vacant alley. Our car's headlights were blinding me, but I could still see what they were shining down on. The kid was coughing up blood and spitting out teeth.

Marty delicately placed the wet drive in his satchel, and he was right to be gentle. The memory of my violent assault was worth more than both of our lifetime earnings to date.

The bleeding jock moaning at my feet had made the mistake of sexually assaulting the daughter of a millionaire software engineer. Now, both father and daughter would have the pleasure of beating the hell out of this kid over and over again, until the memory quality degraded to nothing but picture. After that, they still had a movie to watch from time to time. They had no fear of legal recourse and, in return, Marty and I would touch an income tax bracket that we never thought we would even smell.

He grabbed me by the head and looked into my eyes. "You ok?" He asked. "Are you good? Jesus, you really gave it to him."

When Marty took his hands away from my face, I saw that he had gotten some blood on them. It certainly wasn't mine. That shook me a little, but I didn't let it get far. It was time for act two of the night's performance. I needed to stay focused.

Marty was already on the phone.

"Hi, I need to report a mugging, or-or an assault. I don't know. The man had a bat and—no, I'm fine. I saw from my window. There's a boy down there, he's bleeding really bad."

For a second I thought Marty had taken an acting class without telling me. The longer he talked, the more I realized he was pulling from real anxiety. Real fear, maybe of me.

"Oh, god, there he goes. The man with the bat just got into his car—what? Oh, I don't know. It's—it looks like a green sedan, but it's dark. Wait—wait. X-E-D! Definitely. X-E-D. Those are the first three letters of his license plate, I'm sure of it."

Marty hung up, threw the phone on the ground and stamped on it like it was a leech that he found on his neck. He was sweating. Panting.

Without looking up from the phone, he asked, "Are you ready?"

I wasn't. Act two was always going to be the hardest one, but I had to be ready. I wiped some sweat from my brow, realized it was blood, and told him to plug me in. He handed me a pair of keys, stepped out of sight, and stabbed the needle into my mind.

"Fuck. Fuck! Hold still." Marty sounded stressed. I knew he was rushing. He had to. The implant for act two had to be small enough and hidden away so it didn't turn up on any scans when I was arrested. When the needle-work was done, he stepped back into view and sat across the table from me, dressed as my lawyer.

There we were. The hardest part was behind us.

If he had been unable to get a session of solitary, unsupervised access to me, then the whole car chase memory would have been worthless. A little bit of time in custody was to be expected at the end of a show like the one I had apparently pulled off, but no one wanted to serve an entire sentence in exchange for ten minutes of thrilling entertainment. Which reminded me.

"How long?" I asked.

Marty checked his watch. "Two hours."

"What? No, not 'how long has it been?' I mean the chase. How long did I last?"

My business partner grinned. "Dude. Twenty-five minutes."

My jaw dropped. "Nice," I whispered. This meant our product would be worth twice the cash we expected.

"I know, man. You did good. Let's get to act three before they break this up. Great work, though."

Now, it was time to coast into the biggest payday of all. Some absolutely insane writer was doing research for a crime show. He was so committed to his craft that he wanted to know what it really meant to be "on the inside." He kept his name from us, but I imagine he was pretty big. With the money he was paying, he was working for the sake of art, not income.

Resisting arrest and aggravated assault would buy me five years in a county jail at most. Maybe the writer was crazy, but at least he would come out of his sentence having lost only a couple seconds of life. I would be five years older when it was all said and done. I wondered if I would come out of it with any new aches or pains. Hopefully no one broke my nose while I was in there. Ideally, I would wake up absolutely ripped, with a couple cool tats being my only memory of the place.

Marty and I didn't want to chance waiting for another moment to insert the next implant. Our client wanted to experience court proceedings anyway, for love of screenplays. After some "goodbyes" and "good lucks," my friend and successful business partner pressed the needle into my temple for the last time.

"What?" said a voice that was as dark as the room it inhabited.

"Look," someone else said. "He's already rigged."

As if the concern over the lack of Marty's voice wasn't enough, my body was suddenly crushed with pain. My muscles were weak. My joints ached. My eyes—

Opened.

A woman with short hair—and by the look in her eyes a shorter temper—was looking through me from only a foot away. The angle suggested that I was laying down, but my sense of orientation was still covering up the truth.

"Let me guess," she said. "You don't remember a god damn thing."

I shook my head, despite my stiff neck.

"That's amazing," she said, seeming to mean it. She looked up towards someone that I couldn't see. "Can you believe that?"

"Looks like an older model. Slipped right past scans all these years."

All these years, I thought. I immediately wondered what had gone wrong, and by how far I overshot my landing.

"What happened?" I asked.

My voice sounded old, raspy.

"You went to jail. Would you like to rephrase the question?"

The woman almost seemed to be enjoying this.

"Five years," I said. "I was supposed to be in for five."

"Five? Dearest, I hate to break it to you but you've been nestled up for a good *thirty*-five."

"What?" I tried to sit up and felt my arms catch on thick restraints.

"Wait, wait, wait." She leaned really close. "Here comes the real trip. What country are you in right now?"

I responded out of reflex. "America."

She reared back, eyes wide. "Unbelievable. You're a real relic, friend. Unfortunately for you, it's a new country but the same laws regarding Murder One."

I had fancied myself a sort of chess mastermind in the creation of the retirement plan. Now, just like in chess, I saw my mistake before anyone pointed it out.

I let my head drop.

"The kid died in the hospital," I said, hopelessly relaxing into my restraints. "He died in the hospital."

"If you say so," the woman said.

"I'm free to go now?"

She cast an annoyed look to whatever lab tech or assistant was in the room that I couldn't see and sighed.

"Alright. This was explained to you ten minutes ago and I have a busy day ahead of me so I'll have to be brief. Keep quiet, listen, and save your questions for after. Got it?"

I nodded.

"You're thirty-five years into an eighty year sentence, but—"

I groaned and closed my eyes, saving up for screaming and thrashing later.

"*But,*" she said. "Your deteriorating health suggests that you won't make it another year. So before you go, we're going to speed things along and implant the rest of your sentence."

"Ok, slow down," I said.

"Did I not preface this by saying I was going to talk fast?"

"You did, but—"

"*SO,* in your day they couldn't take the memory without you losing it, right?"

I nodded.

"What a relic. What a treasure you are. Since most of the population wears implants these days, the justice agency is able to take a much more 'punishment fits the crime' approach. Now, we can copy instead of cut. So there are *a lot* of memories floating around out there since it doesn't make a difference to the holder, some of which are purchased by the government."

She motioned to the assistant, or whoever he was. He stepped into view, with some kind of new tool. The futuristic version of Marty's needle, I assumed.

Marty.

I wondered what happened to him. How often did he visit me in jail? What did he do with our money?

"The government-controlled memories are used for two things. Investigations and criminal punishment. Bats haven't gone out of style even though no one plays the sport any more. A forty-five year montage of any kind of weapon is a tall order, so most of these will be repeats. There will also be some bare-knuckle experiences in there. No firearms, though."

It was so unceremonious. Before sending me to finish out my sentence by getting beaten to death over and over for forty-five years, the woman simply said, "See you in a few."

"Continued - The Suburbs" by: Arcade Fire

HARBINGER

The historian in the next booth over seemed to be an intense man. Maybe it was just the circumstances. Though I couldn't see the particles of calcium dust, I'm pretty sure he was grinding his teeth into snowdrifts on the table below. He was dictating instructions to the "illustrator" that sat at his side, a man I could only describe by what I could see, a head with a back that was covered in brown hair. This was all I could discern from my vantage point.

Both men were in a frenzy because soon the bar would open to tourists, and any sense of "what had been" would be quickly clobbered with "what is," albeit disguised to the best of its ability. How two men from "is" managed to get behind schedule in the land of "had been," was... well, the universe still has its mysteries, I guess.

The stool I had claimed by the bar wobbled slightly every time I shifted my posture. It was as if the entire room was trying its hardest to make my experience a genuine one. I was seated at the corner of the bar where I had a clean shot at the TV. People had warned me to avoid such a view. Apparently it was easy to fall into the trap of wasting your entire hour simply gawking at whatever was on the screen. I was so regularly pummeled with vibrant projections and obnoxious advertisements back home that I was pretty sure I could avert my eyes from one little two-dimensional LED display.

I felt so god damn privileged to be engulfed in the scene, the snapshot of a tavern just before they dimmed the lights and turned up the music. By way of an emptied savings account, I had made it into these four walls. The fifteen-minute lead time, however, had been by lottery. By stroke of luck, I was able to enjoy my first drink in peace with all natives and no tourists, save the historian and the illustrator.

Any fears I had of buyer's remorse was completely eradicated when I saw my first old guy, or "geezer." Everyone had seen projections of these guys, but I've got to say, they didn't do the wrinkles any justice. I was flabbergasted to be sitting two seats over from a man that was fully aware that his body was decaying, and that soon it would expire. What grim courage he must have had in his heart. When our eyes briefly met, I raised a glass to him. He'll never know the respect I was lifting with that gesture.

There were so many things that the brochure and poorly rendered projections had undersold. From time to time, a moment would be punctuated by the clack of two or six billiard balls. When I walked, my shoes stuck ever so slightly to a floor that must have been pummeled with barrages of spilled drinks over the years. Of course, I knew there would be vintage music, but no one told me how thin the quality would be. It was an awesome surprise. The playback of a song called "Where is My Mind?" was no better than the buzz of a bee compared to the quality I was accustomed to.

The bar counter itself barely earned the phrase "load-bearing structure." Its uneven surface, covered in a plastic sheet made to look like wood, trended towards a general inward lean. Apparently one or two of the other C.G.E.-approved sites actually let people dance on the bar. It wouldn't be happening here, and that was quite alright as far as my interests were concerned.

The Rook Room, as the locals called it, had received its C.G.E. certificate of approval because of how dead-quiet it had been on the night that it was destroyed. Lots of floor space meant lots of room for tourists. As I surveyed the establishment, I wondered how it kept the doors open. There were five customers total, and I knew for a fact that three of them were visitors paying with fake currency, myself included.

I knew that the evening was about to begin when the historian and the illustrator discretely packed their things and left through the back door, subtly tapping their wrists. After that vacating, the final festivities of The Rook Room commenced incrementally, in five-minute intervals, as the precisely timed new arrivals found their places and ordered their drinks.

The bartender died happy, so at least there's that. I'm sure he expected nil in tips on that mundane Monday night. Instead, he received a torrent of business that was no doubt overwhelming, but worth every drop of sweat in the eyes of a working man. I can't be sure how many of the patrons that night were tourists, but none of them had any reason to be stingy, although we were encouraged to avoid throwing money around like darts so as not to raise suspicion.

Those of us who were merely visiting had three signals to identify one another by. The first and least dependable was a nervous-looking scratch at the back of the neck. If we saw this gesture, we were to return it. The second was a pinching of the bridge of the nose, suggesting a rough day, or exhaustion. Again, if we saw this, we were expected to mirror the motion. No one wanted to waste time talking to a fellow tourist. We were here for the genuine article.

Lastly and most dependably, upon shaking hands, the implants in our wrists would give a swift twitch. Apparently physical contact like that was significantly more common before the days of super viruses and bacteria.

Later, outside, I was able to enjoy one of the more bizarre social rituals of the era. The chem-filter that preceded my lungs absorbed all of the carcinogens and nicotine, converting them into energy, which in turn was used to keep the filter ticking. Unfortunately, it did nothing against that sticky, black flavor of cigarette smoke in my mouth.

All part of the experience.

There were four of us out on the sidewalk, puffing away to enhance our social interactions. Two were tourists like myself. I didn't catch their names. There was Stiff-neck, whose discomfort was so radiant that I questioned why he had even booked the trip, and at his side was Blinky, either obsessively cleaning the pollution from his eyes, or struggling to believe what he was seeing.

The fourth member of the smoker square was a native. Craig looked worthy of a microphone in a rock band. His build was a meek one, sharpened by a collage of shattered tattoos, and decorated with a narrow black beard and some piercings. I'll bet Craig was feeling pretty damn interesting for the duration of that smoke.

The strangers with whom he had just become acquainted seemed so curious about his entire life, leading up to this day. The three of us colluded to squeeze modern humor out of him, "shooting the shit" as our trip advisors had called it.

And what a trip Craig was. Seeing him as the forgotten blip that he was about to become hurt in a way. He was performing his little, thoughtless idiosyncrasies for the last time that night, but would never know it. Craig was a guy who would scrape his shoe against the sidewalk and do an about-face just to punctuate a joke. Sometimes, if he wanted to amend something that already had us going, he would lean into the center of the circle and move his hand like he was throwing dice as he spoke. He was a man standing on the ledge of drunkenness, playfully balancing on one foot, tempting the fall and fighting it at the same time.

"My friends always bust my balls about this stuff." He pointed to his various silver ring piercings with the speed of a hummingbird. "We call it the dozens. They'll say 'Your face looks like it can't say no when a guy drops to one knee.' And I'll say, 'No it dozen.'"

Myself and Blinky cracked in friendly laughter, Stiff let loose too, once he caught up.

"Yeah, I've heard all the dozens," Craig said, now indicating his tats. "They say my arm looks like Van Gough wiped his ass with it and I go, 'No it dozen.'" He blew smoke to the sky like a combustion heater.

Either by incredible tact or natural ability, Blinky got us on the subject of the future, and what it might look like. We all let Craig lead the discussion.

"Mars is a dumpster, dude." He swung a slap at the sky, and missed. "We'll get up there in the next decade but it'll just be a dirty, irradiated armpit. Drop some boxes there, maybe a set of spare keys, then we're off to Europa. You heard of that one? It's just a moon but it's got liquid water." His eyes went wide then dropped to a squint in defense of flame that was igniting his second cigarette. "Liquid. Water. That's over half of the freight expenses for the low, low price of 'free.' Just wait. Europa. Our lifetime."

I smiled right past my sentimental sorrow. He didn't say it, but I could tell Craig had spent some time imagining the incredible view of Jupiter that a small cottage on Europa would have. The guy had bright ideas about the future. Not to say that it actually turned out all that dark, but we hadn't made it to Europa yet.

Whether they were bored, depressed, or economic with their vacation time, Stiff and Blinky staggered their way back into the bar. By their grace, I was granted what our trip advisor had called a golden moment, one-on-one time away from the crowd, with a relic of the past. Craig offered a second gross-stick. I scratched my neck to make sure the chem-filter was ready for more. It gave subtle click in response.

"Europa, huh?" I asked. "Would you move there?"

"Fuck yeah."

"Really? One way ticket, you would leave it all behind?"

"It's not about leaving it behind, fr—ah, what was your name again?"

"Jory."

"Yeah, Jory. Sorry." He exhaled my name and the apology with a plume of hazardous chemicals in a polite direction. "It wouldn't be about what I leave behind."

"What about your family?"

"They'd be sad to see me go, but they've got that empathy going on. That means if I'm happy then they're automatically happy. Like a chemical response, dude. As for everything else..." He slapped his hands together, liberating them from imaginary dirt. "My work here is done, man. I think I did a good job. Caused some pain like the rest of us, but net gain in earthly happiness, you know? I could ride a rocket to the sky tomorrow and leave feeling pretty damn satisfied that I did alright while I was here."

That filled a hidden reservoir in my heart. There were no better words to hear from a friendly guy that only had two hours to live. Would I seek out a friendship with a guy like Craig if we existed in the same era? Probably not, and that's what had turned our little interaction to gold. It was a verbal handshake between two different times and lifestyles.

Craig decided he had ruined enough breaths of fresh air, and returned to the warmth of The Rook Room, almost unannounced. Ending the encounter with a lie seemed to cheapen the bond, but I told him I was going to stay outside to make a call. In return, he gave me a salute as he swung his way back into the box of music and laughter.

It was mind-blowing to me that more tourists hadn't made a concerted push to appreciate just a moment outside. Cities of the early twenty-first century had a reputation for being filthy, sure, but drinking and talking could be done in any era. Observing a skyline that was oblivious to its pending annihilation, cars driven by combustion whooshing their way down a quiet street for the last time, breathing in air that would soon turn hot and toxic... those things weren't available at home.

If there was one thought that they had driven into us during orientation, it was to avoid being caught up in the loss that was about to occur. Sorrow made for a bad trip. Every now and then, it caused people to try taking matters into their own hands.

Apparently, in the industry's early days, some tourists would try things like kidnapping a native and making a run for the edge of the blast zone. It would have been a blemish on the permanent records of the human race if *someone* hadn't tried it, even if it was a futile effort.

Now, the company had all kinds of pre-checks and countermeasures to make sure that no one tried to alter the timeline. If just one person made their way out of the city before it was destroyed, it was impossible to tell what effect they could have on the future.

Places like The Rook Room were approved for visits for that exact reason. The natives there had a low flight-risk. By cold hard math, even *if* a tourist managed to convince someone to evacuate the city for their own safety, they wouldn't have enough time to outrun the shockwave.

The implants in our wrists were designed to fry any phone or communication device we touched. To beat the dead horse, travel guides were monitoring all other calls in and out of the city and censoring anything that seemed to contain news from the future. Even if a tourist stole a car and immediately gunned it for the edge of the blast, their location would be tracked and they would be pulled back to our home time. The city was a graveyard waiting to happen, and there was no changing that.

It would be easy for a tourist to feel miserable and powerless in such circumstances, but those personality types weren't in C.G.E.'s typical customer demographic. Most came for a night of no-rules debauchery or a vintage experience. I heard a poem or something once about "The serenity to accept the things I cannot change, the courage to change the ones I can, and the wisdom to know the difference." I wouldn't say many of the tourists were wise, but they seemed to have the serenity thing on lockdown.

I'm not sure what I was looking for when I signed up. Nothing big, I guess, just a collection of little moments. I had heard of premium rewards members that keep coming back, visiting different sites during the same hour. It was a real mind-bender to think that there might be five or six copies of the same person, each a different age, scattered across the city. Someone could be celebrating their thirtieth birthday at The Rook Room one hour before the destruction, then their fortieth taking a stroll in the park.

I wondered if there was an older version of me out there, making a return visit. At that moment, out on the street, I doubted it. I couldn't imagine being able to afford another trip in my lifetime. Before departure, I fortified myself against being one of those people that wanted it to last forever. If you think of the trip as a time or a place, you always want to extend it, or go back. I tried to imagine my stay as a precious stone that I found at my feet. It wasn't like I could find it and put it in my pocket a second time. I could keep it, though, as a memory. That's why I spent the week prior to my departure playing memory games, planning to carry the lost city with me, rather than needing to return.

As tempting as it was to stay on that street and soak in the aroma of a city on the edge of never, I only had a half hour left before I would be ripped from this time, back to my own.

"People," the guide had told me. "It's all about people."

I stepped back inside to make a few more condemned friends.

I couldn't say exactly when I met Sue. The process was piecemeal, a war of attrition. My first and somewhat apt words to her were, "I'm sorry," after I accidentally bumped into her. Hardly a "meet-cute." About ten minutes later, I waved to a friend from my time and Sue was caught in the middle. She apprehensively nodded back, probably wondering if she knew me. We passed each other in the narrow hall leading to the restrooms. I said, "Hi," too quietly to conquer the music. She smiled.

Her hair was set in the classic style of the local time, brown, with waves of a mid-range frequency. Her skin tone was indicative of a cold and cloudy winter, somehow managing to be both warm and pale at the same time. I won't bother trying to describe her eyes with any justice, but I will say they were blue.

Our incremental introduction was marked as a final success when she accidentally accepted the wrong drink, mine, from the bartender. This led to her first words to me, which were also, "I'm sorry." Past those two, I think I managed to catch one third of what she said before we managed to escape the blaring crowd and the sounds of a band called "The Airborne Toxic Event." I had provided the excuse by motioning with one hand, *Cigarette?* Once we got outside, we discovered that neither of us had cigarettes, smoked, or had any intention of starting.

"Maybe some cardio instead?" She gestured down the street, and our first and final stroll commenced. The moment I checked the time, I realized that my healthy mindset was starting to crack. I had fifteen minutes left in my visit, and I had just found a diamond too big for my pockets, one that I wanted to keep finding, over and over again.

"Should we start with names or origins?" I asked, and she let on that there was something funny about the way I asked.

"I was a kid about six hundred miles that way." She pointed vaguely south. "You?"

"New York—upstate, not the city." I had been told that was a safe answer.

"Cool."

"Yeah. Cool." I kicked a chunk of road salt from the sidewalk, back into its territory. "You grabbed my drink on purpose didn't you?"

"Totally." She smiled at her feet.

"You could have just asked."

"I was super parched. It was an urgent matter."

"Dehydration? I'm so sorry, I had no idea."

She let out the dramatic cough of a dying person. "It's ok, we're walking towards a hospital."

Our minds and bodies fell into sync a moment later when we both felt a chill. We had both left our winter wear back at The Rook Room.

"Oh, shit." Sue looked back towards the bar. "Can I wear your T-shirt as a scarf?"

I reached down, threatening a swift removal. "I'll do it."

"Please don't. I'll blush all over the place."

"I hate to break it to you, but you already are."

"It's the cold, not you. Just so we're clear."

"I see. I didn't realize I was strolling with a liar."

She drove her hip into mine, knocking me out into the street. I'm not sure how she made an attack feel intimate, but she did. I stood my ground on the pavement, looking up and down the vacant street.

"I could have been hit by a car, you know. What then?"

"Hospital. Remember?"

"Good call." I snuck a gander at the time as our walked resumed. The report was not a good one. As much as it sucked, I put some forethought into how I would make my exit. It would be rude to vanish right before her eyes, but if I couldn't come up with a reason to part ways then I might have been forced to spend my last few minutes saying goodbye.

Would I tell her what was about to happen?

It was a question I had put endless thought into prior to departure. Did convincing someone of their imminent, inevitable death improve or ruin the time leading up to it? The decision I had arrived at was, *if* I said anything, it would be a simple nudge in the direction of living to the fullest for the forty-five minutes that followed my departure and preceded their demise, without mentioning the death part.

"Where did you just go?" she asked, snapping me out of my calculations.

"I have a dog at home and I just realized I forgot to feed him." Lying again, cheapening the evening.

"A dog? What's his name?"

"Ah, Sedgwick."

"Interesting name. What breed?"

"British. British bull hound." The hole was getting deep. The corner was getting closer to my back.

"I never heard of that one."

"Maybe you should get cultured. Read a book or something."

She smiled and tried knocking me into the street a second time. I caught her in an awkward, accidental hug. Another diamond that I couldn't take back with me. She lingered there just long enough to crush me with fear that she was drunk, that her warmth and playfulness were chemical instead of genuine.

I righted her back onto her own two feet. "So do you come from a big family?"

"I have a request," she said. "Only talk about the present and future."

"Ok. What do you do for a living?"

"Nothing about work, either."

"Ok, ok, I got it. Where do you see yourself in five years?"

She furrowed her brow. "Maybe I should ask the questions."

"Yeah. Do that." I stifled the urge to rub my bare and freezing arms.

"This is a lightning round, so get ready. Snow or rain?"

"Snow, of course."

"You obviously forgot about the thunder."

"Nope. I stand by my statement." I remained tight-lipped.

"Alright then. Summer or winter?"

"Summer."

"Ah, a walking contradiction. Coffee or tea?"

I had never tasted either. "Coffee."

"Popcorn or ice cream?"

"Pass."

"*What?* On both?" She seemed deeply offended.

"On the question. Too close to call."

"Fine. Sunrise or sunset?"

"Rise, for sure."

"Why?"

"I don't know." I surrendered my strong image to the cold and blew warm breath into my hands. "Potential?"

"Road trip or visiting a new country?"

"Both, at the same time."

"You're such a cheater. Pick one."

"Visit a country, I guess."

"Good choice. Top or bottom?"

The sound I made was a mix of "uh," "hey." She was almost certainly drunk. Good at hiding it, but drunk; unless sexual dynamics were regarded more casually in this era.

"I'm kidding, don't answer that. It's your turn."

The timer in my ocular implant confirmed that my turn would be a short one. We had three minutes left. I needed to soften whatever blow my sudden disappearance was going to cause. "Ok, but new game. What are the three things you would do if you knew you were going to die in the next hour?"

"Eat sushi, kiss a stranger, go double the speed limit. You?"

"I see you've thought about this before."

"Duh. Now you go."

"Hang on, the game isn't over. In a couple minutes, I'm going to do a magic trick. If I pull it off, you have to go do those things."

"What if we hit someone? I'm not in the mood for vehicular manslaughter."

The fact that she said "we" made me want to die with her. She had assumed I would be joining her for all three. My whole plan started breaking down when I realized the act of vanishing would be insanely hurtful. Now the truth was roaring inside of me.

One minute to go.

"I can't do this," I said. "So, you won't believe any of this yet but my magic trick is going to be a disappearing act. It's completely against my will and I would love to stay, but I just can't. What's important is that you do those three things and have a blast doing them without me." Then, absentmindedly, I bookended our brief encounter with the same words. "I'm sorry."

I knew when she smiled that there was no convincing her, not until I was gone. "Jory," she said. "It's fine."

I checked the time to see if there was any time left to kiss her while still being a gentleman about it. My heart collapsed in on itself.

They were supposed to extract me twelve seconds ago. Even that infinitesimal delay meant catastrophe when it came to a trip like this. It was a time-travel vacation company. They could be running six days behind on their end and still pull me out right on schedule. By nature, it was impossible for C.G.E. to be late.

"Hey," Sue put her surprisingly warm hands on my cheeks, helping me focus. "It's ok."

Jory, you idiot.

I hadn't done any of the proper checks, and accidentally spent my entire trip with another tourist. I quickly but delicately grabbed her hand, but the implant in my wrist failed to give a confirmation. The entire system must have broken somehow. Maybe I had wandered off some kind of grid.

"I have to get back." I repeated that a few times. Broken, looping.

"You will, don't worry." She was chasing me now. We were both riding the thin divide between walking and running.

"No, you don't understand. I'm late. I was supposed to be gone. I can't stay."

"Jory! I know for a fact that you're going to make it out just fine."

It was the second time she invoked my name, which reminded me I had never given it to her.

"How do you know my name?"

She answered it with a warm hug. I could feel her voice vibrating into me when she said, "Because I was too big to fit in your pocket."

My next words floated on the current of an easy breath. "I came back."

She nodded into my shoulder then pulled away. "You couldn't get enough, you big idiot."

"But why pretend?"

"We actually have a bet to see if you can figure that one out on your own."

"A bet? How much?"

"One dollar. Fake or real, depending on who wins."

"Ok. Tell me this," I said, pretending to challenge her. "Whatever is happening here, if we keep walking could we screw it up? In terms of timelines, I mean."

"To put it in your words, 'we're already swimming in paradox.' I don't think the screw gets any looser than that."

I put one foot in front of the other, and started figuring out how to earn my dollar.

It was like being out of bounds, or out past curfew. I was a kid again, in a way. Dropping from my bedroom window after dark to meet *the girl*. To set me further at ease, Sue played out the old time-travel proof standby of telling me a few of my most intimate secrets. Those five minutes were obligatory, no matter how well adapted I was to the idea of slipping between decades.

"You used the same thing on me," she said. "Earlier this evening. Now get to the bet."

"You have to give me a little more."

"Nope. You have to work with what you have. We agreed."

"How do I know?"

"Because you said you already trusted me by now."

She had me at such a disadvantage. I started assembling a mental puzzle, out loud. "You took your time getting to me at the bar. Because... I told you to?"

"Very good. And..."

"And I was worried that if you rushed things, it would ruin it for me?"

"The word I would use is paranoid, not worried, but yeah." She quickly offered a dollar. "It's been waiting in my pocket for you since we met."

I tried to refuse, but she insisted. "A deal's a deal."

Taking my winnings, I asked, "How long have you known me?"

"About three hours."

I mouthed a "Wow." Three hours was an expensive amount of time. "So I'm rich in my future?"

"You told me not to give you any details about that. Again, paranoid."

"Future-me sounds frustrating."

"A little. He's not here right now if you want to break the rules a little."

"Let's do it. Just a little."

"Does this mean you'll give me shit for it the next time around?"

Next time around, I thought. "Sue. I'm getting really confused."

Without further delay, she started shedding some details. In my future, I would make two return visits, working my way backwards through her timeline. Even as a bonafide time traveler, it took me a little to comprehend all of the implications that such a relationship involved.

With each trip, I went a little deeper into Sue's past. The visits were years apart from my perspective, and hours in reverse from hers. She met me for the first time when I was older, and now I was meeting her for the first time at my youngest. When I started to reason out why things had to go so inconveniently backwards, I couldn't think about anything else.

Going forward in her time was impossible because there was no forward, no later. In less than an hour, there would be no Sue, no city.

"There's that sadness," she said.

"So, I told you what—"

"No, and you told me to stop you if you tried."

That one didn't seem fair, and I said so. She countered.

"I think I already figured it out anyway. Knowing details would just make it harder to ignore." She turned away from me, and the topic at hand. "Anyway. Coffee?" I heard the jangling of keys as she unlocked the door of an old brick apartment building.

"I, uh. You already know I say yes, right?"

"Nope. Everything since your planned departure is new. When we first met, or when I first met you, you said you were going to try and extend your first trip."

"I can do that?"

As we stepped inside, she said, "You weren't sure, but apparently you found a way."

Climbing three flights of narrow stairs to her apartment was enough to melt the winter freeze from my nerves.

"Oh, almost forgot." She reached to the top of the doorframe and grabbed a spare key. "This is for trip number two. It'll make things easier. One of the few 'Jory-Approved Edits.'" She said the last words like they were the title of a five-star theater performance.

Her place was uncomfortably small. She offered "the tour," claiming that it would save me time later. She managed proper introductions to her bathroom, kitchen, and bedroom. At that door, I had to ask.

"Have we done, uh, that?" I pointed to the bed. "Just curious."

She smiled and closed the door.

I followed her to the kitchen, pleading. "No, no, I didn't mean tonight. Or, this hour, or trip. I meant later, or earlier. You know what I mean."

She was scooping coffee grounds into one of the archaic, plastic appliances I had seen in projections. "Your second trip. It's when we both knew each other the longest. We could do it again if you wanted."

"Oh no, no it's fine. I'll wait."

"Are you sure? We're talking years from your perspective."

"I'm patient."

"Consistently." She handed me a cup of hot darkness. "Although you were pretty quick for a time traveler."

"Please don't say things like that." I burned my lip on the coffee, making my first experience with actual, real coffee both painful and repulsive. "So what do we do now?"

"I already told you, I don't know. This is all new."

"No, I mean what should we do?"

"Oh, well we did two of my three. Ate sushi on trip two, kissed you on your third trip because you were still a stranger. Go for a drive? No pressure. I mean it's my last time seeing you so you should be really accommodating, but it's totally fine if you're afraid."

Sue's screams of joy were no match for the sound of her car's redlining engine. When we maxed out at one hundred and ten miles per hour, my paranoia bloomed. What if we hit someone? We would only be killing them a little ahead of schedule, sure, that was the logic of it. But the emotion was, it was still murder, no matter how good the timing.

"Stop, stop, ok!"

She eased down, gracefully. "Wow. That was ridiculous."

"Satisfied?"

"Absolutely."

When the car squeaked to a halt at the first of four red lights we acknowledged, I finally put a confusing question to words.

"What if we got into an accident and I was paralyzed or something?"

"Oh my god." She looked like she had just dropped and shattered a beautiful ice sculpture. Shocked and guilty. "You might not make your second or third trip. Oh man, don't let me do that next time."

"I can't, I'll be me."

"No, not now, I mean your second trip then. Tell me not to risk it. I'll be a little annoyed. Actually tell me not to bring it up because you will try to make me happy by doing it anyway."

"It worked out ok this time."

"I know." She shifted in her seat to face me, like a comic-book super fan excited to talk about something that no one else understood. "Ok, so we have a theory. Your first date was different this time because you told me to make changes, right?"

"Wait, this is a date?"

"Shut up. So the theory is each loop is affected by the one before it. Like, we can pass ideas from one to the next. Since this is my third time seeing you, but only your first, I can tell you things to bring to your second meeting."

"Then on my third, I tell you everything we learned."

"Exactly," she said. "It's not just a constant, identical loop. We can pass stuff on and make little changes each time."

"So we're crafting the perfect night."

"Better every time."

My mind tumbled. "How many renditions do you think we've had?"

"No way of knowing. Oh! Maybe we should start counting."

"That's great. Hand off the numbers." A breath of silence let me ponder the idea. "Actually."

"Yeah you're right," she said preemptively. "That takes away from it. Is there anything we should change next time around?"

"Absolutely nothing." When the romantic words dissipated, I adjusted. "Well, okay. There were a few times that I got sad because you seemed a little too drunk."

"Oh." Her gaze left me, wandering elsewhere. "Well, you don't tell me. I mean, not me-me. Because." She shrugged. "End of the road."

"I'm so sorry. This is your last hour with me."

"Depends on how you look at it I guess. Trip two. Tell me on trip two."

In that moment, I wondered if I actually would. Those moments on our walk were downs. They made the ups even sweeter. I don't know how I broke free of that moment to check the time, but when I did, Sue intervened.

"Don't worry." She extended her hand, revealing a small, rounded, black cube. "I fibbed a little. This is how you're here past your departure. You made it, I guess. Go ahead, you can touch it."

I pinched it out of her palm and brought it in for a closer look. "It keeps me here?"

"You called it an inhibitor. As long as it's within ten feet. It blocks the signal, or whatever pulls you back. When it's time to go, just throw it away. Since I gave you the idea this time, I have to tell you the idea behind it."

"Keeping me here longer."

"Not just that. If we ever have some kind of mental meltdown over trapping different versions of ourselves in a date loop, we could just keep you here until after..." She ran out of words.

"After I need to go." I wondered if she knew what that meant. It would be murder on her part and suicide on mine to stay, a real Romeo and Juliet tragedy.

"But I would never do it," my Juliet from the past said. "I think you just made it to give us, like, a security blanket. In case I freak out or have some existential crisis. Maybe I already did and you wanted to give me the option. I don't know. It sounds ridiculous because it's only a four hour relationship and it's new every time, so obviously there would be no reason to—"

I kissed her, for my first time.

I couldn't say exactly when Sue said goodbye. The process was piecemeal, a war of attrition. First, she laughed a little less, but still seemed happy, just in a different way. We spent our last ten minutes on a park bench, listening to some of Sue's favorite songs off of her phone. We agreed not to discuss them too much so we could "nerd out" about them later.

It didn't feel cold any more.

"On your next trip…" she rested her head on my shoulder. "Can you tell me to make sure we do this again?"

"Does that mean you're not dumping me?"

She gave me a shove, reached into her pocket, and produced the tiny cube that was keeping me right when I wanted to be. "Holding you here means killing you, doesn't it? That's how the cycle would break?"

I nodded. She looked to the sky.

"So it's something big?"

"I thought you didn't want to know."

"You're right. Sorry."

I think both of us were about to ask the question. "How much longer?" It was cut off by a beeping sound, and a red blinking light shining its way through the skin on my wrist.

Sue reared away from me like I was a bomb. "What does that mean?"

"I didn't tell you already?"

"Not this time. I would appreciate a warning next round, though."

"Sorry. It's the one minute warning."

"Oh." She got close and laid her head back on my shoulder. "How close do you want to cut it?"

"I'm still young and reckless. Wait till the ten second countdown?"

"You're sure it has one?"

"Oh yeah. It's really dramatic. How far can you throw?"

"More than ten feet."

Then came a few streaks of sparkling flame across the sky. Each one quickly died, leaving only a trail of smoke through the atmosphere. Their numbers grew, as did their size, as did the prominence of the light above.

I felt a stab of pain when I looked at Sue and saw that she was afraid. It would be the most brilliant meteor shower of her life, but she couldn't enjoy it. Next time, I would warn her. There had to be a way to make her final moments better than these.

The first of ten beeps invaded the moment. We were seconds away from the catastrophic impact that ended it all. Suddenly I was afraid, too. Three more beeps passed, and Sue sat motionless.

"Sue?"

"I know. Do we say 'I Love You?' now?"

"I don't think we're ready for that."

"You're right." She snuggled closer.

Two more beeps. Sue gave me a swift kiss on the cheek, said thank you, and threw the cube as far as she could just as the sky switched to daylight.

When I appeared at the arrival gate, no one seemed aware of my tampering.

"Let me be the first to welcome you back from your once-in-a-lifetime journey with Chicago Getaway Experience," a greeter said. I realized there were tears in my eyes and wiped them away. When the greeter didn't acknowledge them, I knew he wasn't even real. Human renderings were still pretty far off from the real thing.

"Deactivate projection," I said, and my optical implant erased the well-dressed man from view. Then a loudspeaker blared a significantly less friendly voice.

"PLEASE VACATE THE PLATFORM FOR THE NEXT ARRIVAL."

I stepped off just as another tourist flickered into existence behind me. He was absolutely wasted and obviously had spent his entire visit at The Rook Room. Actual humans hurried to help him to a chair. Drunk returnees were all-to-common.

On the train ride back, there was a malfunction that added a half hour to the trip. I didn't mind. Returning to regular life sounded like a terrible inevitability.

When I transferred lines in Phoenix, I received an auditory notification that my checking account was overdrawn. I told the virtual banker to transfer funds from my savings, but there was nothing left, thanks to my little journey. Thoughts of money reminded me of my souvenirs. I pulled out the dollar that I had won in my bet through time with Sue.

Looking closer, I saw that it wasn't a native dollar. She had given me a counterfeit from my own time, a prop used by tourists to have a good time. My previous iteration must have lost some other bet. The bill looked a little worn around the edges, but the fakes were made that way so they could hold up to scrutiny. I wondered how many times she and I had passed on the same fake currency, each time knowing that we tricked the other into taking it back. It was a game of tag that only one of us knew we were playing at any given moment.

Life eventually fell back in step, like it's meant to after the loss of a loved one. That's the closest feeling I can compare it to, but it was obviously more complicated than that. There was a growing glimmer in there, since I knew that somehow I would find a way back to her and that doomed but beautiful city. I looked at the key to Sue's apartment, and wondered when I would have the privilege of using it.

It was endless layers of bittersweet. She was a light at the end of the tunnel, but her very existence turned my entire life into a waiting game. Waiting to save up the cash for another visit.

I pinched pennies for a year and made next to no progress. There was always something that set me back. Eventually I wised up, switched strategies, and started applying for entry-level jobs at C.G.E. Determination brought success.

Being an intern sucked. Greeter sucked even harder. I climbed the ladder over the course of two years. During that time, I met a girl named Vera. Loving her made me feel guilty. Eventually, I spilled, telling her about Sue as a matter of sheer necessity. I was honest about my intentions, too. Vera and I stuck it out for a while, but eventually we were pulled apart by a girl that died eighty years ago, in Old Chicago.

My moment finally came when I mastered basic imitation intelligence coding. After three years of waiting, it only took three weeks for me to plan my move. I reprogrammed the nightly custodial droid to recognize my face and grant me access to the departure gates. It worked flawlessly.

I met Sue at the sushi place she had described during my first trip. I realized that this could be my best trip of the three. She had already met me, and I her. I started by getting disappointments out of the way. I had only liked about a third of the songs she played for me in our final hour. We argued playfully for a little, pretending subjective things were objective, then started off our packed agenda.

"I hope your wait wasn't too long," she said, earnestly as we enjoyed some   sushi in a city that was just a little too far from the ocean.

"About three years. Could you maybe warn me next time?"

"No can do. What if you did things differently and couldn't make it back?"

"You could give me instructions. Like a schedule to follow."

She looked at me like I was an idiot. "Do you really want to spend our time dictating your past three years so I can memorize them? Do people in your time still say if it ain't broken don't fix it? Wait, why aren't you eating?"

"It tastes like low tide. Maybe we do a different place next time?"

She slumped in her seat. "This is my favorite spot."

"Ok, sorry. Forget I said it."

The mood felt irreparably depressed until she smiled and kicked me in the shin, a concealed attack beneath the table.

"I said I was sorry!"

She smiled. "I know. And now you won't call my dinner 'low tide' next time. Or do I have that backwards?"

"I think. Yeah, you'll have to tell younger me to pretend I love it."

"God. I just don't get it." She was talking with a full mouth but concealing it behind her hand. "If I tell you to pretend you like the food, things should change, right? Then how come it still happened?" Off of my confusion, she said, "Right, sorry. No paradox talk. Sorry."

"Don't be sorry. Can we get some other technical stuff out of the way really quick?"

"Sure," she said, still chewing. "Shoot."

I warned her off from ripping around in her car the next time she saw me, citing the risks of breaking the loop prematurely. She called me paranoid. I made her promise. We moved on. I delicately asked if she would let me tell her what happens to her after I left, just to minimize the fear. She refused.

The rest of the trip was an absolute dream. We went back to her place, where she began a frantic pocket and purse quest for her missing key. I let her sweat it out for just a few seconds before producing the one she had given me on my first trip.

"Apparently you left them inside on our first-*first* date. You told me I had to kick the door in that time. We've been handing this off ever since."

"We're pretty smart," she said.

"I know. Brilliant, really." Before stepping inside, I left the key on top of the door frame, for Future-Sue to give to Past-Me. Trip two was so simple on the personal level, but so confusing on the timeline level. Both of us were passing ideas and objects to former and future versions of each other, but not experiencing the changes that they should cause.

Then came the torrent of things that all meant the same thing. A shrug. A nervous laugh. A cheesy joke. An offer of coffee. All of this to say:

Well... here we are.

I felt like the bedroom itself was lurking somewhere in the shadows, right over my shoulder. Every traditional, soft surface, for that matter was shouting "You two should kiss!" like the obnoxious, drunk, and clueless friend with a proficiency for spoiling all darling moments.

Having been trained in the ways of the times, I asked, "Do we put on music or something?"

"Sure, or the TV." The silence that fell as she looked for the remote arrived as a downpour. "How do they do it where you come from?"

"The same as you. There are all kinds of ways to enhance the sensation but they're basically biological drugs. Programmed viruses and—"

"No, I meant the culture, not the act. You have to have something better than TV."

I felt like we were standing in different rooms. "Sorry. Yeah, we have things in our eyes, implants. We can set them to show both of us the same projection. If you can afford a good one it can change the whole room into a beach or something.

"Interesting."

"Yeah." I cleared my throat. "Interesting."

As if a lightning bolt came down from heaven, we both burst into laughter over our mutual discomfort. Then came the confessions. We learned that neither of us could ever put "smooth" on our resume.

"Maybe we just shouldn't," I said.

"True. I could just get you when you're younger anyway."

"I didn't want to last time. It was too fast."

"Oh, like now?"

"Kind of." Our giggles met somewhere between us. "On your third trip, when I first met you, you told me we did it. Were you lying?"

"I don't know."

I did some thinking. "I think I'm going to regret this, but maybe we should wait."

She warned me that there would be absolutely no carnal pleasures on my next trip. I assumed that was because my third "date" would be her first. The solution presented itself in a frustrating way. We could orchestrate a better mood, but not until the next loop. Neither of us would get to experience or remember it, but we would be doing ourselves a solid.

We would each tell the other the truth. No sex. Next time around, the expectation would be gone. Instead of a preordained obligation, maybe it would feel more natural.

The entire room relaxed, and we settled in to watching a film made by Michel Gondry, some French director that must have been lost to the sands of time. Sue laid her legs over mine, and that was nice enough. We shifted closer, and my arm went over her shoulders. We started to lean, and eventually fell into a position that still, across time, is called "spooning." Then came kissing, then came touching, then came the unstoppable force that we failed to stand against.

Near the end of my second trip with Sue, it felt like I was walking her home, though it was quite the opposite. She had never been to The Rook Room before, so I showed her the way. As we strolled, I told her what must have been our usual briefing.

"Take your time meeting me. Last time was perfect."

"What did I do? No, never mind. I'll just do what feels right."

"Good call. There's just one thing, if you don't mind."

"If you don't mind," she said in a deep, mocking tone. "I think we're past niceties."

"Fine. Listen here, wench. When you play the lighting round game with me, maybe leave out the 'top or bottom' question. It made me think you were just drunk and lonely."

"That's sweet, but what's the lightning round game?"

As I explained it to her, my mind nearly burst over the idea that the game of questions had been my idea all along.

"Oh, that's great." She added a little one-two hop in her step. "Fun."

We turned a corner and saw, of all people, my younger self. I was standing outside, talking with Craig. The scene was unfolding about a block away, and we had no problem ducking out of view.

"We're early." The gloom in my voice surprised even me.

"This is hard for you, isn't it?"

"Passing off my girlfriend to a younger man? Yeah."

"Oh, we're using titles now?"

Her lips gave mine no chance to answer.

A few minutes later, like a true, early twenty-first century gentleman, I walked her right up to the Rook's front door. Sue told me where to find her on my next trip. It was a nice touch, and I appreciated the poetry that she had orchestrated.

"Try not to be so creepy this time," she said.

"How do I do that?"

"You'll figure it out."

I savored the kiss that would be my last for an unknown amount of time. Our hands were slow to part ways. My first three steps away landed on the cold sidewalk, my fourth landed in the future.

There were three guards with taser rifles pointed at me when I arrived at my own time. Getting into the building had been simple, but apparently unauthorized trips were easy to detect. Although my departure from Chicago had been right on-time, my return was automatically delayed by three minutes, which allowed security enough leeway to make an immediate response. My job termination was instantaneous. I spent three days in jail before being sentenced to eighty hours of lunar mining service and slapped with a fine equal to about half of what used to be my annual salary.

"Endangering Temporal Continuity" was a very serious crime. If I had intentionally tampered with anything, I would have been looking at time in prison. Lucky me.

Machines took care of all the digging, cutting, blasting, and refining on the moon. Obviously, there was no heavy lifting involved in my punishment. The real penance was the horribly mundane hours of supervising equipment that almost never failed. All of my implants were disabled, limiting my stimulation to a grey horizon, a control panel, and an employer that could speak directly into my ear no matter where I was.

When my service was up, I returned planetside, sold everything I owned, and moved into basic-income housing. The government provided me with what was officially called "essentials" and what the rest of the world called "bum pay." Unfortunately, I needed more than that to pay off my fine. I got a telemarketing job and worked seven days a week with the occasional double-shift. I was good at it. The job security was solid, since the very idea of imitated intelligence with enough of a human touch to call and harass people seemed pretty far off.

I paid off my debt in three years and got a better job in another two. It took spending eight hours a day on my feet, trying to upsell customers that had strayed a little too far into the sales floor of an implant company called "Gateway Tech." It paid well enough that my Bum Pay benefits were cut, so I just about broke even. Still, it felt good to be independent again.

Through everything, the hateful screams on the phone, the vandals in my neighborhood, having my tiny bank account hacked, I never forgot about Sue. Most nights, I kicked myself for not coming back with a picture of her hidden in my shoe. Something. Anything.

I met a girl named Tera at work about seven years after saying goodbye to Sue. Before her, I had been surviving on bondless flings and the occasional rental doll. Tera and I eventually moved in together. I loved her, and I was honest with her, keeping no secrets except one. That secret was Sue. If the relationship was to end, I figured it best to let something in the present do the damage, not the past.

The secret was made easier to keep when C.G.E. closed its doors and liquidated all hardware of any value. The company had remained financially stable by selling five-minute visits at bargain prices as a way of preventing Chicago from being over-saturated with tourists. It was the change in temporal law that really brought the behemoth company to its knees. Trips were taxed heavily and eventually deemed illegal. The historic case of one "Jory Amper" was brought up many times during all legal proceedings. My only claim to fame.

It was both unbelievable and ironic. Somehow, by getting arrested for endangering temporal continuity, I had altered the future. The technology was dead, seemingly tipped over the edge by one man's transgression, done in the name of love. Thanks to this twist in history, I never designed or purchased the inhibitor that kept me at Sue's side on the first trip.

Tera and I married and had two sons. Guilt struck from time to time, which of course is absurd. Even twenty years after my final kiss with Sue, I felt like I was cheating on her. In a way, I was. I had called her my girlfriend, but never broken up with her. I think there are some things that we have to tell ourselves, mandatory beliefs that, if removed, would drive us insane. Mine was that my ex-girlfriend named Sue had died, which terminated our emotional-contract. This was also true. She was simultaneously alive and dead.

Tera and I were happy, but humble. Neither of us could afford regeneration therapy and we were already turning grey. One night, over drinks with my son, I told him about Sue. I can't say for sure why I finally burst open. It was most likely because I didn't want her memory to die when I did. Fathers and sons play catch all the time. I think more often than not the elders make a permanent pass in the form of a thought rather than a ball. I hope he caught that one and held onto it.

Mankind made its first footprint on Europa over one hundred years after the death of a small, frenetic, bearded man named Craig that often fantasized about living there with a killer view of Jupiter. I knew I would never be able to afford the trip, but I did purchase a small holographic projector that rendered a three-dimensional oil painting of the vista. That was one of the few items that I held onto when Tera and I moved into the nursing home with the rest of the people that couldn't afford regeneration.

On her deathbed, Tera could only whisper the words, "Don't feel guilty." I took her hand, leaned close, and asked her what she meant. "Craig has a surprise for you." The name was another legacy, passed from father to son. It's obvious now, but at the time I couldn't fathom what kind of gift would come with guilt. Tera solved the mystery for me. "If you don't meet Sue, you don't meet me. Go talk to your son."

Her final words before the curtains closed on her life were those the undying, romantic tradition. I don't think the phrase "I love you" will wear out before mankind does.

Craig had gone his entire life holding a secret of his own. Although the official story was that he was working a mundane maintenance job at the capitol, he was in fact one of five people in the world that was aware of the government's only remaining, and quite illegal time gate.

"It's too risky." These were my first words to my secretive son. "They'll lock you up."

He countered by saying it was better than never existing at all. I tried to explain to him how much more complicated it was than that, but only came off as a babbling old man, especially considering Craig's line of work. He was the expert, now.

My son had yet to love, so he was mobile. He informed me of his plans to abuse his power, skip ahead a few years, and retire someplace quiet, like Europa. Funny how those things work out.

This would be a one-way trip for me, considering what had happened on my last return. That would be fine. I had spent enough time living in the past that dying there seemed incredibly apt.

I refused to leave until I could hug every living member of my extended family. Although Craig had remained solo, my other son turned out to be quite prolific as far as bringing new life into the world was concerned. I taught his five-year-old how to spell "Chicago" before leaving.

We didn't even need to sneak into the facility in the middle of the night. My son had done well for himself, and ascended the hierarchy well enough that no one questioned him. As I stepped onto the platform, Craig handed me what I immediately recognized as the breakup cube. I had described it to him the same night I told him about Sue. Since there was no other way for me to know about such a device, he knew in that moment that he would be the one to give it to me.

My final thirty seconds in my native time were more thrilling than any spy simulator I had ever experienced. Craig informed me that on his way out, he would be sabotaging the gate. It was illegal for any nation to have one, anyway. There would be no one looking for little old me, so I wasn't the one that needed the inhibitor. It was a gift, an extra forty-five minutes, for my youngest self.

I was one hundred and sixteen years old when I returned to Chicago for my final trip. Sue was right where she told me she would be. It was the same park bench that had supported her final moments with me, beneath the raining fire. She was engrossed in her phone and didn't bother looking up when I asked if I could take a seat beside her.

"Boy," I said, groaning over my aching joints. "What a sunset."

She smiled and put her phone away in an effort to entertain a tired old man that was looking for conversation.

"I was just thinking that," she said. "Lucky us."

"Lucky us," I agreed. "Miss, I don't want to be creepy, but I have a couple things to say to you. I promise I won't take too much of your time."

The final trip was a lot of work for me. It was mostly set up, the standard trust game of reciting Sue's personal secrets. This in and of itself was a minefield. Some secrets are off limits when it comes to convincing someone you know them. I had to avoid all things that said *I know where you live,* or *I've seen you naked.* Fortunately, my non-threatening nature was a huge boon in this effort. That is to say, she knew she could outrun me if things got too strange.

It wasn't just a process of debate and logic, though, and I soon realized that I was wooing her. Delicately, I plucked away at her humor strings. It felt just as good for me then as it had years ago.

It took thirty minutes, half of my visit, to put her at ease and bring her to a place where she considered believing what I was telling her, all that to continue a loop that I would no longer be a part of. This was my time to spin off.

"This may be a stupid question," she said as we walked beneath the leafless trees. We were linked arm in arm and she was helping me along. "But why are you doing it backwards?"

Despite nearly one hundred years, I had yet to prepare an answer to that question. The babbling old man within me came out again. Eventually, I refined my thoughts and answered with two words. "Something happens."

"Something?"

"You've never wanted to know what it is."

"It's something bad? For me or you?"

I shrugged, and her furrowed brow showed that she was going to crack the case.

"You're here. So it's bad for me," she said, glumly. Always a source of levity, she added, "*If* I believe any of this."

"That reminds me." I coughed a little. "Could you return me to an old folks' home? I have some other women I would like to creep on."

"Oh, really? You know all of their intimate secrets, too?"

I nodded. "My life's work."

The sun was gone and the twilight was on its deathbed. Now lit by amber streetlights, I finally saw Sue as I remembered her.

"Ok, I have one more question," she said.

"There's no limit."

"You know the future. Is it all set in stone?"

"We don't think so."

She released a one-beat laugh, musing. "You said 'we.'"

"Of course, we talk about it a lot. We've never tested it. Want to try?"

"How would we do that?"

"Well, for example, I'll bet you one dollar that you don't have the courage to actually kiss a stranger."

She was so fast, and I suddenly felt the warmth of a nice peck on the cheek. "There," she said. "One out of three. My future, my choice."

I gave her the dollar that had changed hands between us countless times, surviving centuries.

We were close to the sushi restaurant, now, and I knew our time together was at an end. For me, this wouldn't be our typical "see you next time around." It was goodbye for me, hello for her. Despite all of my best efforts, she didn't quite seem to be convinced that we had both been caught, spiraling, in the shape of a double helix through time. I can't blame her for her skepticism, but I knew I was going to feel miserably bitter leaving without her trust.

She brought us to a stop. "How do I know this isn't just some set up for a younger buddy of yours? How do I know it's you in there?"

I had no way to answer it. No identical scar to point to. No secret that couldn't have been shared in some prior conspiratorial meeting. My feeble mind struggled to recall that second date from so many years ago. There had been something strange about the way she was looking at me. I originally assumed it was wild infatuation, but now I knew the truth. She was studying me. For an unknown amount of time on my second trip, Sue had been trying to decide if she believed me.

"You'll have to look into my eyes," I said.

So soon, it was time for my grand finale with Sue to end. There had been no speeding car, no lovemaking, no drinking. I suppose old men and first dates go hand in hand.

"What happens now?" She asked. Her next encounter with me was just around the corner.

"Wait," I said. "Please wait, just one more minute. You need to take this." I held out the inhibitor cube with a shaking hand and explained its purpose, an extra forty-five minutes tacked on to my first visit. "Don't tell me about it until I start panicking about being late. Ok? I really like the way we met."

Sue eyed it suspiciously before finally taking it. "So when I walk away from you," she laid a hand on my chest, confirming that she was talking about Jory three-point-oh. "You disappear?"

"Yes," I lied. Telling her about my one-way ticket would garner too much sympathy. She might opt to stay with the lonely old man, trapped in a time before his own.

"Then this is goodbye?"

"That depends on how you look at the guy waiting around the corner. Would you treat me to one more hug?"

She did, and added a peck on the cheek. As she walked away, I turned and began to hobble towards my final destination.

Two seats down the bar, a young man did a horrible job concealing the fact that he was analyzing my face. He had never seen an old man up close before, as people from his time could throw their money away in exchange for eternal youth. I could just barely remember sitting in his chair, looking at the old man beside me, studying his wrinkles.

Our eyes met and we each raised a glass to one another.

Courage. I remembered thinking that the old man was courageous for living in a frail body. If I had any intention of altering the course of my youngest night in Chicago, I would walk right up to the kid and tell him, "Not courageous kid, just dead-broke."

Everything in The Rook Room seemed just a bit less than what I remembered. Either my memory had enhanced the place over the years, or my age and fading senses had blunted its finer edges. I sat there for a good while, watching TV and keeping to myself. The Rook wouldn't be a bad place to go, not bad at all. The fear that everyone had was of dying alone, right? Things here were just getting started.

Sadly, it wasn't in the cards for me. My younger self wouldn't recognize me, but Sue would. It was just about time to get gone. I saw good old Craig come blundering through the front door, the recipient of the final gift I had to give.

A short while later and no thanks to my weak legs, I made it to the restroom just before my bearded, tattooed friend. I pretended to be washing my hands just as he walked in.

"Your name is Craig, right?" There's something about wrinkles and grey hair that gives you a free pass for being assertive in odd places. The pass was doubled by Craig's loosened state.

"Have we met?"

"We have a mutual friend," I said with a smile. Taking a gamble, I tossed him the gift. He caught it. "That's a present from him to you."

The young guy was too put off to ask what it was. I patted him on the shoulder on my way out. Before the door could close, I saw light bursting out of the restroom. Craig had activated the holographic projector and been treated to a three-dimensional, animated oil painting of a beautiful view from the cliffs of Europa.

"Holy shi—"

The door closed.

I saw Sue enter through the front and made my exit through the back, into the alley.

Cold and tired, I started a search for a diner, anywhere I could warm up and enjoy a bowl of soup before the city was erased from the surface of the Earth. That was the exact moment that I realized there was a major flaw in my plan. I had come without so much of a cent in my pocket.

So this is what it feels like to be homeless.

It was going to be a long couple of hours, and I would spend them bouncing between gas stations and convenience stores, pretending to shop in exchange for just a little bit of heat.

As it turned out, I couldn't bring myself to go indoors. Something about cowering in the warmth felt disrespectful to the condemned city. As long as I kept walking, the worst of the cold would be mitigated. I took my time exploring streets that I had missed during previous trips, appreciated architecture, and took deep breaths of the air.

"You had a great run," I said to the skyline. "Thanks for the visit."

What a strange place it was, unique, perhaps to the entire universe. It was the city that experienced a sudden and mysterious boom in its population, flooded with curious strangers that then vanished as quickly as they had arrived. This was a place that was treated to one unexpectedly lively Monday night, just before closing time. The serenity was broken by the tremendous, strained roaring of Sue's car. I watched it rush by and out of sight in a matter of seconds.

Kids these days.

Soon our piecemeal goodbye would begin.

My fond acceptance of the new loop was suddenly shattered by a mere snowflake, then a second, and a third. My memory had been hazy but there was one thing of which I was absolutely certain. It had not been snowing the first time I said goodbye to Sue.

Yet, from above, an increasing number of large, fluffy flakes were falling. There had been a change, and not one that could possibly have been perpetrated by two young lovers.

The weather.

The weather itself had been altered. A whole storm system that didn't exist in the first loop was now silently blanketing the city of Chicago. My understanding of paradox finally began to mature. We had been making so many changes to our own past without feeling the effects in the present. I spent my entire life accepting it as an indecipherable mystery of the universe. Now it was clear. The answer to the mystery was that it wasn't contained within one universe.

We had been editing parallel renditions of the world. Each successive loop was independent of the previous one. In this universe, this reality, the sky had said "to hell with it," and released some frozen moisture. If such massive, meteorological phenomena could change from loop to loop...

I moved my feet as fast as I could, starting a painful shuffle in the direction of Sue's racing car, towards the park. My legs, already tired and cold, were just about useless. Even staying upright was a struggle. Though my knowledge of the city's layout was a touch hazy, I knew that I had a hopelessly long distance to travel.

A car approached. I turned, waved, and desperately shouted at it, or tried to. I only coughed, instead. Hunched and convulsing, I continued my agonizing push towards the park bench that began and ended my relationship with Sue.

If the weather had changed here, it was possible that the path of the meteor had been altered as well. Some fleck of dust, billions of years ago, might have escaped the gravity of a passing comet, going left instead of right. Maybe a star somewhere was never born. Little green men could have crashed their spaceship into an asteroid. The Earth's orbit could be an infinitesimal amount slower or faster. Anything, any minor change to this universe could prevent the impact that killed the city.

In this rendition, this universe, my younger self could stay.

The air forced my lungs to do more coughing than breathing. It was yet another loop in my life: stinging, wheezing inhale and violent exhale. The streets were so god damn empty and what cars did pass simply ignored the waving homeless man on the sidewalk.

I fell, and managed to shout in anger at the sidewalk beneath me. When I finally got to my feet, my shuffle was downgraded to a limp.

"HELP!" The shout was a whisper. "PLEASE."

Never had I felt so alone, and I wondered how long it would take for the tears on my cheek to turn to ice. A welcome numbness came over me, reducing my pain only slightly. When I was a mere three or four blocks away, an ache in my left arm spread into what felt like a clenched fist in my chest. My heart was failing.

I saw them.

Two silhouettes, seated, and waiting for a timer to run down. I didn't know what time it was. Couldn't be bothered with it. With five minutes or five seconds to spare, I would be going the same dreadfully slow speed.

Clutching my chest, I pressed on. It was difficult to tell, but I could have sworn that Sue looked my way, ever so briefly. Had she seen me? Put the pieces together? Most dire of all, had she seen the same hobbling old man in previous iterations? Ignored him? Had it all happened before?

The fist in my chest turned to a knife. Something about that pain pushed me to yell, truly yell, defeating the raspy whisper that had crippled me thus far. I went down, landing hard on my shoulder. My weakness was so overwhelming that I couldn't even turn to see my young self down the street.

The sadness I felt wasn't for this iteration of myself. I was to die no matter what. It was that young couple on the bench. The girl that was about to throw a small piece of technology just over ten feet, sending the boy she loved back to where he had come from. It would have been nice to spare them both the sense of loss, save the boy from a difficult life.

That would have so been nice.

My thoughts were snapped in two by a familiar sound. It was the one-minute warning before impact, but it wasn't coming from me. The young couple had run to my aid. This was new. This was good. In lieu of my absent words, I reached for Sue's pocket. Of the two, she was the only one that would recognize me.

I lacked the dexterity to grab the inhibitor, but Sue took my meaning and handed it to me. I pressed my hand against young Jory's chest. Through a terrible haze and disorientation, I could barely tell if he understood what I was telling him. Both of them were shouting, frantic, asking questions that my voice couldn't answer.

The ten-second countdown began, and Sue took the cube back, pointing far.

"Throw it?" she asked.

I grunted angrily, grasping for the cube. She handed it back to me. I clasped my weak hands around it, and my younger self tried prying them apart. I growled at him, the little idiot.

The beeping countdown ended with a sustained, five-second tone, and then there was silence, nothing falling from the sky but those fluffy, prophetic flakes. No streaking fire, no destructive boom.

For a second time, I pressed the inhibitor into my younger self. Pushing him.

You. I thought, but couldn't say. *Yours. Stay.*

He took my hand in both of his and retrieved the inhibitor, that little precious gem that I had brought him. He put it in his pocket, where I assume it stayed for a long time.

Tears in the Rain - Hans Zimmer

THE INDUSTRY

Let's face it; the industry just isn't what it used to be. There was a time, not ninety years ago, that I could close four edits in a single day. Yes, I'm serious.

"If you could change one thing about yourself," I would ask, "what would it be?"

This was my hook for about a century. I'm not saying that every meeting I took was a sale. No, there was plenty of rejection, but the sheer volume of demand was so large that I could label my first three brunches of each day as warm-up runs.

I could sit at a table with someone for two minutes and know if they were a buyer or a walker. If they even asked about a price tag, they were all mine. Anyone who could boil the idea of a genome edit down to a simple integer had already made the biggest mental leap.

After sixty years of milk and honey, the slow decline set in. The naturalists like to take responsibility for the slump. They certainly gave it their best. At the height of the movement you couldn't go one week without seeing a crowd of wrinkled protesters or a lone, obese idealist on the corner, preaching about the beauty of nature.

They all thought they were bringing down the editing industry, but the truth was that the market was simply shrinking. All of the adjusted people were passing perfect genes onto perfect kids. Sure, there was a small crowd for second and third generation kids that wanted to be edited down to less-than perfect, but the percentage was negligible. It was just a fad.

With the sharp decline in cosmetic edit sales, age reductions became my lifeboat. My commission on those was a mere fraction of what I could make on a total genetic overhaul, but at least it was something.

So then, how was I supposed to sell a miracle edit if I didn't look like an absolute marvel? Staying young was an expensive part of the job, but there wasn't any way around it. My overhead was holding a knife to my throat.

If I couldn't make enough sales, I couldn't afford another age reduction. If I aged, my chances of selling would only drop. It was literally an ugly spiral; I had seen it happen to a number of colleagues over the century. One day they would look to be in their late twenties; the next, I was skipping their funeral.

Then came the bone-dry year. Not a single sale, and not for lack of trying. I begged friends of friends to introduce me to acquaintances who were cosmetically challenged. I floated out the prospect, smooth as butter, but each time I was turned down. The market was saturated.

I had to change my tactics. I just didn't know how. I'm not sure what about this one lady inspired the idea, but I can tell you the exact meeting that gave birth to my new business model. Now, I know I can't prove this, but I will bet you I was the first agent in the business to take this new approach.

Marcie Powers was her name. I still remember the account number, one-one-seven-oh-two-nine-nine. I ought to get it tattooed on my thigh. She couldn't afford a rocket blast up to me, so we wound up meeting on the surface, some holographic café in New York.

Sizing her up wasn't difficult. Her face was cute, her hair was full-bodied, and her teeth were well seated. The only two things: she had about thirty pounds that needed losing and a few early wrinkles on the way. Most of my pitches were to forty-year-olds. She was right on that target.

The café windows displayed digital images of pre-submersion New York. I could see well-rendered taxicabs and pedestrians meandering below. It was a pretty view, but I knew it would distract her from my pitch, so I chose a table near the counter.

I danced around the subject for a while, working instead on making her blush.

"You don't need this!" I yelled, "Go buy a boat instead. You're beautiful!"

She didn't blush, but she laughed, and that was close enough.

"Does it change the way you think?" she asked. It was a heavy question to open on.

If you woke up with a different face, would you act differently? You bet. Now, what's the difference between how you act and how you think? Don't ask me, I'm just a salesman.

"Not unless you want it to," I answered. "But Marcie, I'll be honest with you. I've seen some really messed up people that needed brain stem alteration and you aren't one of them. In fact, it would be a sin to mess with your personality."

"I have a friend who made a few cosmetic changes," she confessed. "Just freckles, and she wanted to be a little taller. She seems a little different now."

"People who have finally found a way to love themselves are often difficult to recognize," I said, nothing dishonest about that. I know plenty of people who got fixed up and found themselves hanging with a different crowd. It's a natural side-effect, usually a positive one.

"Does she seem happy?" I asked, projecting a level of empathy more believable than the digitally-rendered yellow cabs zipping around outside on streets that were actually submerged in thirty feet of filthy water.

"I guess so," she said, and I could see in her eyes she was flashing back to a good friendship that had since dissipated. It was clear that Marcie was the type of girl that couldn't emotionally accept the idea that not all friendships are eternal. Life is long. Most friends stick around until it's inconvenient. I had to bite my tongue to keep from imparting that wisdom upon her. We were supposed to be talking about positive things.

The meeting was all wrong. We had gone down a road of negativity. I did my best to redirect the flow back into the light.

"Guess how old I am," I said.

"Oh, it's impossible to tell." She flexed her labored smile, lifting the added weight of her plump cheeks to above-average height. Few people in the solar system can smile and still look sad; Marcie was one of those gems.

"Just a guess. Please, you won't offend me."

"I couldn't begin to."

I was only testing her. It's a great question to ask someone if you want to gauge their risk-taking potential. Of course no one could ever guess right. The range is too wide. The fact is, if they aren't willing to try, they aren't going to blow their savings on an edit.

"Really, please. Could you just tell me?" she pleaded.

"I'll be one hundred and sixty-four this July." I smiled, wanting nothing more than to shake her.

Yes, it was true. Back then I was only a century and a few quarters old. Every day of my life after thirty was spent as a poster child for genome edits. From what I understand there aren't many people who keep age reducing as long as I have. Some run out of money; others run out of interest. Not me. I really see no need to die these days unless you're being murdered. You won't find me in the grave without a knife in my back.

"How do you do it?" she asked, "Don't you have a family?" Normally, people look up to my youth. They admire it. They want it. Marcie took it to family. I had the face of eternal love at first sight and she was wondering if I had settled down with it. All of my tricks seemed to have a reverse effect on her. I knew then that even if I made the sale, which was doubtful, poor Marcie would never be happy. She was inclined to utter sadsappery forever.

"Sure do!" I said. "We take reductions and edits every year, my wife, son, and I. I'll tell you it's weird having a little boy that looks your age."

"I'll bet," she said, more put off by the idea than anyone who had ever heard it. The whole image was a lie, of course. Karlie left me a buck and a quarter ago. She fell behind on her reductions and died the natural way, the unnecessary way.

"Did you want to talk about the change you're looking to make?" I asked reluctantly, just wishing she had been excited enough to bring it up herself. What made it more painful was, I knew she wanted to be convinced, I just couldn't figure out how to give her that service.

"No, I'm sorry to waste your time. I just don't think I could."

I had never bounced back from the word *no*. Once that curse was released, it was like last call at any bar. The fun was over, the lights were up, and I was going home alone.

I thought that was it. End of game. Lucky for me, she moved slowly. That gave me all the time I needed to have the epiphany that would change the industry forever. After this meeting, I would go on to teach underground seminars. Rental edits would spike in popularity. Agents would go to jail for taking things too far. The government even considered regulating or banning our work for a time. Blame me or thank me, I saved the industry.

"Just one second," I said, stopping her. "I'd like to call you and follow up in a week. Would that be ok?"

She agreed, probably just trying to be polite, and made her departure.

I stayed in the café for a solid hour after that, debating. It wasn't an easy choice, so don't go making me out to be a monster. I was looking down the rifled barrel of my own ugly spiral. Age begets failure, and failure begets age.

So here was Marcie, a lady on the way to improving her life and saving mine. All she needed was a little push. I could leave now and call her from orbit next Monday, or I could stick around and help her make the decision.

I canceled my return blast and checked into a cheap surface-motel. That was Monday.

Tuesday, I figured out where Marcie lived. I got a deal on a cheap rental edit. It was nothing flashy, just a generic handsome artist-type look.

Wednesday, the rental edit started to take form. My nose was shrinking, my eyes turned blue and my hair was on its way to being red. I spent the day indoors, signing Marcie up for swimwear subscriptions.

Thursday, I found Marcie's dating account, made one for myself, and asked her out to dinner.

Friday night was our date. My rental edit's effects were peaking. I was a good-looking, bearded redhead. Marcie and I ate dinner. Holograms all around created the illusion that we were floating in orbit at some kind of upscale American restaurant.

I turned on the charm. I asked questions. I leaned in when she spoke. I can't be sure but I think I manually willed an actual sparkle into my eyes. I laughed at her jokes. I even paid for the whole affair.

At her doorstep, I started debating exactly how far I would take the date. Luckily, she made the call for me. The moment for her to invite me inside came and went with no such offer being mentioned.

Before I walked away, she asked if she would see me again.

"Marcie," I said, "I had a really fun time tonight. I've been going back and forth in my mind but, I'm sorry, I just don't think I could move past our age difference."

I watched her posture deteriorate. I could tell she was hurting on the inside. The space where she had stored her fantasies of our bright future was now empty. I had planted the seed of a void.

"I'm sorry," I fibbed. "I hope that's not a mean thing to say. I just don't want to be dishonest."

"No, of course not. It's good to be honest," she said, barely. "Thank you for dinner."

I marveled at the maturity with which Marcie had taken her rejection.

Saturday, I bribed a twelve-year-old boy to run up to Marcie and call her fat.

Sunday, I panicked just a little. The rental was taking a while to wear off. I continuously rubbed the face I couldn't recognize.

Monday, my natural face returned. I called Marcie. She wasted no time, immediately inquiring about weight edits and age reduction.

For the duration of the phone call, I could barely listen to a word that Marcie said.

I was in a dream world, having cracked the code of a new business era.

I imagined the whole of humanity packed into a ball of rough clay and saw the ball smoothed, baked, and shined into a perfect sphere.

I saw myself accepting awards for raising the low-end of society to perfect equilibrium with the rest of us.

I envisioned an entire race of flawless, intelligent beings spreading amongst the stars.

I talked Marcie through the varied packages that were available. Some came with included eye-color change and natural minty-breath alterations. She didn't seem to care about the add-ons. All she wanted to know was the price tag. I gave her the integer she was looking for.

"Truth" – by: Alex Ebert

DRAG

Cynthia smacked, howled, and screamed against the outside of Todd Barrett's motel room window that night. Times like these, he was glad he hadn't fully committed to "tramping" and bought himself a fifth-wheel. Sleeping in a camper on a night like this would have been impossible. Instead, he had a soft bed below him, a strong roof above, and a simply superb on-demand adult video channel buzzing before him.

Three months prior, Todd had completed his apprenticeship. Now, he was a full-blown honest-to-no-one lineman. FP&L was shuffling him everywhere in the great state of Florida to keep the electricity flowing. Sometimes it was faulty wiring, but most times, the times Todd liked best, he was hiking up power poles and repairing the damage from Mother Nature's worst.

Whenever bad weather was on the rise, Todd went out to location prior to the worst of it so he could get to restoring power early the next morning. If Cynthia truly evolved into the horrible raving bitch of a hurricane she was predicted to be, he would have his work cut out for him. He looked forward to the morning. Powerless cities were quieter, the smell of freshly snapped trees was often in the air, and despite the destruction, the birds usually went right on singing.

With a bright surge of light in his motel room, the entire building's electrical system was choked out. Todd Barrett's all-time favorite lesbian porn flick vanished from the screen.

I should get to sleep anyway, he thought, but before he could close his eyes, they were flooded with a blue light that could have competed with the sun. The blue turned to orange, and through his second story window, Todd could see a deluge of sparks raining down in the motel parking lot.

As he stepped to the window, another burst of sparks ejected from the transformer above the lot. If not for the rain, the un-trimmed hedges below would have been set ablaze. In the brief light he saw—did he?—it could have been someone down there in the center of the parking lot. Todd wasn't sure until a third spray of particulate fire illuminated the property. It was a man in a white T-shirt and basketball shorts. He was curled up in the fetal position, nested in one of the lot's many neglected potholes. It was as if he had mistaken the muddy rain puddle for his bed, coiled up and fallen asleep right there. He wasn't moving but— was he screaming? It was tough to tell over the storm and through the window.

Now came the most ancient of debates, to help or turn away. Todd groaned a mellow "oh, shit," when he realized he had already made the decision. He was supposed to be a good man. He had told himself he would be making all the right changes ever since his mouth had gotten him into trouble. Todd had a knack for talking, usually about others, and often about things they considered personal. Since his black eye from last week, he would drink less beer, help more, hurt less, shut his mouth, and hopefully find a good honest woman some time soon.

Todd threw on his raincoat and left the room in a hurry. In all likelihood, the sudden electrical flash had temporarily blinded this poor bastard that ran out to his car to retrieve his forgotten toothbrush or something. Todd had seen what an overload could do to a person up close, and they were still plenty dangerous from afar.

The motel clerk was gone from her desk, though he saw her flashlight moving in the back office. "Hey, someone's hurt out there," he hollered, but heard no reply. Todd pressed the emergency release on the automatic sliding doors, and stepped out into the rain.

Cynthia was indeed an ill-tempered, wild lunatic of a storm. Her winds tried to possess Todd. He was soaked instantly; his jeans probably wouldn't dry for three days. He slowly approached the motionless pile of a man, who was now face down in the flooding parking lot. As Todd drew nearer, some part of him questioned what form of temporary blindness would cause a man to scream into mud like this.

He suddenly realized the error in his assumption that this wet, screaming mess had been a tenant of the motel. Maybe he was a roving crack addict or escapee from some kind of institution. The thought completely froze Todd's outreached hand, but he pushed through the freeze—he was here, wasn't he?

"You're okay," were the first, most natural, and least accurate words to Todd's lips, but they were lost to the wind. He repeated them, this time yelling, "You're ok!" and finally his hand touched the man's sopping, cold, cotton shirt. The screaming man rolled over and his yelling was quickly reduced to a gurgle through the witch's brew of mud, rain, saliva, and blood in his mouth. Todd saw the dirty red fluid streaking from all corners of the man's face, digging miniscule gullies into the mud and gravel stuck there.

Two bloodshot eyes, tucked within that filthy mask, searched wide and eventually locked with Todd's. The gurgling stopped, and the man aggressively inhaled, no doubt taking in some rainwater, then painfully coughed and wheezed. That was when, from behind Todd, the transformer on the offending power pole breathed fire again, and Todd turned to look at it. What he saw there was no mere utility structure.

Something was clinging to the top of the pole. Mother nature's light show had stirred up by now, and the thing— whatever it was—occasionally appeared silhouetted by jagged strikes of lightning in the sky. The first thought into Todd's mind, of all things, was that this thing was something from a hellish crossover episode between *The Muppet Show* and *The Twilight Zone.* Its four limbs were of such lanky length that they looked as though only a puppeteer's wire could move them.

Another flash of lighting brought more unwanted detail. Tufts of hair covered the monster's impossibly skinny form. It lacked elbows and knees, instead utilizing a slow arcing bend of its slender limbs. The thing was doing something up there. Todd watched in disbelief as the nightmare's almost perfectly spherical head parted into a gaping mouth with canine teeth, and sank them into the transformer. Another blast of sparks was set loose. It looked to be feeding on the power grid.

In perhaps a more delayed reaction than Todd had ever experienced, he began stuttering and repeating the only word his mind seemed to have on hand, "No, no, no, NO!"

The creature halted its feast. It heard him. Its eyes opened, intense and glowing.

In two seconds, Todd would make the absolute greatest mistake of his life. As those infernal, luminous eyes swept their surroundings like headlights, and the rain fell like ocean waves, Todd could have run away, but he didn't. Crippled by his own fear, he could only stare. The evil eyes found Todd, and he looked back into them.

Everything... *changed.*

His arms were raised above his head. He heard a plastic, grating sound and felt sharp pain at the back of his head. Todd did not suddenly become aware of the situation, but rather felt it slowly envelop him. He was being dragged down the street. The plastic grating had been the rubbing of asphalt on his raincoat. The pain behind his head was that same rugged surface scratching into his scalp.

It was a bright, moonlit night. Cynthia was long gone from wherever he was now. He raised his head to see the horrible, lanky creature pulling him along by the ankle in slow, lumbering movements. It was much taller than it had initially appeared when beheld at a distance. The thing was maybe nine feet tall, those skinny, jointless legs making up most of the height. Its head hung low, and its free arm slowly swayed to and fro with each step. The creature's open, radiant eyes were lighting the way.

Todd actually spent a moment debating whether or not he should play dead. Next he considered that he was likely as good as dead if he didn't do something. He started with shouting, then kicking, twisting, rolling, and palming his hands into the surface of the street. His nails dug into the asphalt and were sanded down, along with his now bloodied fingertips. Recoiling his captured leg, he aimed to gain ground and attack the monster head on. It was out of reach. After summoning a mountain of willpower, he reached for the disgusting hand that was grasping his ankle. He felt a static shock as he touched its dark, matted fur, and pried with all his might, but could not break the grip. The thing, despite Todd's violent rebellion, trudged on.

Todd tucked his shirt and raincoat into his pants and tightened his belt, trying to keep his outer layers from wrinkling upward and exposing his bare back to the passing ground. He slowly regained his wits and took in his surroundings. The neighborhood was quiet. It seemed there was no one here to help him. The cars looked older. He didn't see a single one that looked newer than nineteen seventy. Over the course of a dreadful two minutes Todd recognized, double checked, and reconfirmed that he was in fact being dragged through the neighborhood in which he had grown up.

He was pulled around a bend, turning onto old Wilkie Avenue. At the end of this street would be a cul-de-sac. At the center of that would be his childhood home. Todd leaned and contorted, trying to see past his captor and catch a glimpse of their destination.

All along the street, his former neighbors stepped out onto their various yards and porches. Each person's flesh had changed, head to toe, into that same muddy, bleeding mixture he had beheld in the parking lot. They went about their daily lives despite the grotesque transformation. Mr. Davis pressed his thumb over the end of a hose and sprayed grass clippings off of his sidewalk. Karly Mason, dressed in her now darkly soiled pink tutu, performed pirouettes and pliés for the world to admire. Todd tried not to look.

His miserable guided tour continued, up the curb, across the driveway, onto the porch and through the front door of his childhood home. As the creature lumbered up the flight of stairs towards the second floor, Todd grabbed hold of the banister and squeezed with everything he had. The creature pulled so hard, Todd thought his leg might rip from its socket. The pain forced him to let go.

Up the green-carpeted stairs, and down the second floor hallway he went. He knew whose bedroom was at the end, and as he was pulled into it, he observed muddied, bleeding versions of both his parents. They were pressed up against the wall, wildly trying to conceive his younger brother, all to the beat of The O'Jay's *"Love Train,"* which was blaring from the very walls. It was his favorite song. Not anymore. He screamed, flipped, and kicked but couldn't seem to close his eyes.

He shouted for his horrible, gangling tour guide to stop, commanded, asked, pleaded, and lastly begged. The creature showed no signs of even hearing him as it stepped out the second story window, dragging a now crying Todd with it. He was pulled out, to his surprise, not onto the roof, but the dirty surface of his old school yard. He watched the imaginary battles of his youth turn real, as each of his mud-caked, bleeding friends were slaughtered by one another.

By what could have been called the second day of being dragged—though time did not exist in this place—Todd had already seen most every location he once cherished. He was dragged through the '64 Chevy Station Wagon in which he had received his first blowjob. He made a hot lap around his high school while listening to *"Love Train"* and watching a disgusting rendition of his old football team gnaw out each other's muddy throats.

Todd's raincoat had mostly withered to Swiss cheese at this point, and his cotton undershirt didn't provide much protection from the ground's coarse sandpaper effect. He resorted to sitting up, entrusting his rugged jeans to hold up at least twice as long as the jacket. He and his silent captor had just about completely caught up on his life by now, and Todd assumed an end of some kind was close at hand.

On the third day of the dragging, Tom was pulled out of the dark motel room that he wished he had never left. He was brought through the lobby, out into the rain, and past the screaming man he had hoped to help. Beyond that, everything turned bright. The rain stopped, and Todd finally felt the sun on his face. To either side of him, he saw vast, endless lines of wavy dunes. It was a desert that existed somewhere outside of his own memory.

On the fifth day, his entire upper layer of clothing had completely worn away. Grating, hot sand grinded into his wounds and formed a layer of bloody paste around him. If he had tried to scream, his dry throat would have yielded no sound. The sun burned his face and chest to the point of blistering. The sand rubbed his back down to mere muscle. It also seemed that hunger existed in this place, though it could not kill. Todd's mind failed him, as he began thrashing wildly, no longer hoping to escape, but letting out his rage and trying to distract from the pain.

Day ten approached, and the dunes rolled on. Todd's rag of a body was pulled past the rusting hulk of an old Lockheed airliner, the decaying hull of a cargo ship, and a few other scraps of metal that his weak eyes couldn't identify. Above, in the tauntingly blue sky, Todd observed a ringed planet, hosting a family of several moons.

"Love Train," rolled on, echoing unstoppably from deep within his mind. He turned over, opting to let the ceaseless sun destroy his back, which had been stripped of its nerve endings. He braced for the grating pain of sand on his wretchedly burned chest.

By the fifteenth day, Todd's muscles had been stripped past the point of use. The lost muscle mass left him thin and stringy, more closely resembling his captor than any human. Thirty pounds of flesh had been shredded away from his miserable body. Knowing he should have been long dead by now, he wondered what he had done to deserve what he feared would be an eternity of senseless agony.

On day twenty, Todd suspected that by tomorrow, he would lose his mind entirely, and that might be good. He was well on his way to ending up just like—

His feeble mind stopped, reversed course, and retraced its steps. *He would end up just like the man in the parking lot— Insane.* In a merciful flash, Todd understood it all so clearly. This creature wasn't something told of around a campfire. He had never heard a single word spoken about such a monster— Why? This had all started the moment he locked eyes with this terrible creature. He had seen it, and it knew he had. Todd had never heard of the monster because no one who saw it could ever speak of it—or anything—again. It was a secret. Now, for witnessing that secret, Todd was being driven insane.

He struggled to form the words with his brittle lips, but couldn't. There was no way for his vocal cords to produce a sound. He tried anyway. If mouthing the four words was all he could do, he would do so for the rest of his tour.

I won't tell anyone, he said, though it was really more a thought than spoken word, and a remarkable thing happened.

The creature stopped.

Todd felt his own foot drop into the sand. The creature, gangly, yet somehow graceful, crawled right over top of him. Through its disgusting dark tufts of fur, Todd could see what might have been eyes; they peered deeper into him than any human eyes ever could.

The creature grunted, stood, and from Todd's perspective, its towering form was never so apparent. It turned, and lumbered away, off into the endless dunes. The creature could not whistle as it walked; the wind did so for it.

Todd was alone now, lying there in that blasted desert, somewhere outside the realm of rationality where pain met time. A sudden breeze kicked sand into his eyes. His decaying fingers curled and gripped the sand to find that it was now wet, and not sand but mud. Water, sweet cooling water, fell onto his wounds and flowed in all around him.

He was no longer in the dune, but laying in the motel parking lot, next to the screaming man. How long had that poor bastard been dragged for looking where he shouldn't? A hundred days? A thousand years?

Above Todd, in a weightless perch on the power lines, was the creature. It blinked once at him, spread its limbs, and caught a gale of Cynthia's wind.

With one flash of lightning, Todd saw the silhouette of that hellish puppet disappear into the thunderclouds. He wondered if he was the only one to have laid eyes on the being and survived with half his mind, or if there were others that shared his secret.

He would never know.

For the rest of his dark, broken life, Todd would never speak of the monster that almost cost him his sanity with a single glance.

The world's most ancient secret went on unheard of, riding the winds of violent storms until wind itself was no more.

"Wolf Suite Pt. 1" by: Danny Elfman

THE ANALYSIS OF A CHOICE

"COMMENCE."

A skewering pain in my leg injected me with a horrible reminder of my mortality. I wondered where my thoughts and memories would go when I ceased to exist, and what would happen to the remaining members of my team when my mind shut down forever. The anti-defeatist part of me spoke up. I was dealing with a matter of "if," not "when." It was a survival scenario.

My training kicked in; I assessed the situation. Compound fracture of left tibia. Moderate blood loss and blurred vision—possible occipital lobe damage. Cardiovascular system: looking good. Despite the non-fatal nature of my wound, the likelihood of my survival was low. I had my environment to thank for that.

The red dunes, instead of stretching out beyond sight, towered over me, forming a small amphitheater of dehydration, sun poisoning, and eventual death. I felt like a grain of rice at the bottom of a clay bowl. Even if I did manage to scramble to the peak of the sandy slopes around me, I knew based on the last four days of our expedition that there was a significant buffer of red sand between us and our salvation.

It didn't take a physician to see that half of our six-person team was already dead. One of the deceased was somehow frozen solid, despite the fiercely burning sun overhead. The ice wasn't even melting yet. Another team member was burned black, still smoking. The third had been impaled through his heart by a lone piece of unknown debris that had fallen from the sky. The bizarre variety of death flavors wasn't of concern at the time. I only cared about the two surviving team members.

I was consumed with guilt when I considered Captain Baker's survival over the rest of the team to be a blessing. Her survival skills were top-notch, her knowledge of first-aid invaluable, and her leadership had already kept us marching far beyond our assumed capabilities. She was unconscious, but showed no signs of other injury.

The second survivor, also unconscious, was Jay, Captain Baker's son. He had about two years before he would hit the rebellious cliff of puberty. For now, though, he was clinging to the evaporating features of youth. We spent a lot of time together, and had recently upgraded our playtime activities from checkers to chess. Although he had no business being on a trek as dangerous as this, his mother had insisted that he join, claiming that "adventure builds character."

My assessment of the situation concluded with damned awful news. Captain Baker and her son were sinking—no—being pulled into the sand. Whether the cause was soil density, a pitcher plant-like entity, or carnivorous fauna, I couldn't be sure.

The decision presented itself in full detail with surprising speed. Baker and her son were equidistant from me, but in opposite directions. I had one ammonia packet, which could snap a human to consciousness immediately upon being inhaled. Either survivor could be awakened, but by the time I crawled to one, the other would have been pulled under and suffocated. It was a common philosophical dilemma. Which one should be saved?

I didn't deliberate over this—dare I call it classic—decision for any longer than a millisecond. My mind got the job done in short order. I immediately distilled my options to their greatest simplicity. The Captain, being thirty-three years older than her son, had less of a life to live but would increase the odds of my survival. Jay had less value in terms of survival, but equated to a major gain in human life and potential, because of his young age.

Other Considerations:

The Captain's treatment of my wounds may have no effect on our situation, and we could both perish anyway.

Jay, if allowed to survive, could grow up to become a killer.

The Captain was partially to blame for our predicament.

Jay would require more fluid intake to survive.

Final influence:

I didn't want to kill a child.

I pulled my ammonia packet from my shirt pocket and crawled, not without horrible pain, towards the young boy. He had already been consumed up to his mid-chest by the dunes. I remained flat on my stomach, covering a wider surface area and preventing myself from being pulled beneath the red, grainy land.

I snapped the packet and held it under Jay's nose. As he inhaled, the gas irritated various membranes in his respiratory system. His eyes snapped open.

"GOD DAMMIT," a voice said, but it wasn't Jay's. It exploded from high and wide, not from the sky, but *as* the sky.

"GOD DAMMIT, THOMAS," the sky said, again.

The red dunes melted away. The Captain melted away. The rest of the crew melted away. Jay melted away. The pain in my leg melted away.

As my vast library of memories and programming returned, I nestled into my old, familiar, virtual environment.

"What is it with you?" the boss asked. When I didn't respond, he took a breath to calm himself. "Sorry. Thomas, please confirm your current build number."

"Version two-point-oh-point-five," I said with my completely disembodied voice. No more legs, no more arms, no more human face. Being an expensive metal box with a personality isn't as bad as it sounds. "Most recent update installed thirty minutes prior to ninety-seventh simulation."

"Great," Boss said, his tone suggesting my response was anything but great. "Now tell me what went wrong."

"A sub-reality error occurred."

"Christ, enough with the sub-realities." I detected anger in his voice.

"I'm sorry, Boss."

"It's fine. Elaborate on sub-reality."

"Records experienced heavy degradation," I said with the sorrowful tone that I had learned from talking to a number of humans. "Minimal details available on the sub-reality."

"Yeah, I figured," he said. "Tell me what you remember."

I started by describing the environment and the condition of my human body. The sand, the broken leg.

"That's a new one." He was typing everything I said.

"Yes it is, Boss."

He finished typing. "Go on."

"The only other remaining records indicate a dilemma involving unconscious victims that were about to be pulled beneath the sand."

"Great," he said, really meaning it this time. Zero sarcasm. "Reviving and suffocation. Very good. We're getting closer to reality. Anything else?"

"All other sub-reality logs degraded beyond accessibility."

"Thomas, can we please stop referring to them as sub-realities?" Boss had a tendency to let minor issues agitate him.

"How should I re-designate them, Boss?"

"Call them dreams. That's what they are." He sounded thankful for this minor and irrelevant breakthrough.

"Will do, Boss."

"Now, can you access any logs recorded outside of this stupid sub-reality."

"Do you mean dream, Boss?"

"YES."

"All logs accessible," I replied.

"Review simulation log."

I prepared the information in an orderly, intuitive fashion, then began my report.

"While cruising in hibernation mode, my vessel suffered a catastrophic collision with unknown space debris. I was brought online to assess damage and take action if necessary. Self-diagnostic showed that my propulsion systems had been reduced to fifty-five percent efficiency. Twenty percent of vessel's power conduits had been disrupted. All other systems nominal."

"That's right," Boss said. "And the cargo?"

"The collision resulted in a sixty percent loss of colonists and crew. Forward hull suffered explosive decompression, instantly freezing 905 colonists. Fires in dorsal and aft hibernation modules caused 1,216 deaths. Piercing impacts of high-speed external debris throughout the vessel resulted in 813 deaths due to various tissue-damaging injuries and cryo-failure."

"So far, so good, Thomas."

"Thank you, Boss."

"Continue." He sounded anticipatory, hopeful.

"Oxygen and power limitations required one of the two remaining hibernation modules to be jettisoned in order to maintain the other survivors. Jettison process of module one would result in a point-three-five percent course altera—"

"I know about the physics, Thomas. Get to what I want to hear."

"What do you want to hear, Boss?" I loved playing dumb.

"Tell me the contents of the modules."

"Module one contained the majority of the ship's vital crew and a small percentage of surviving colonists," I said, wishing I could be more accurate but knowing that Boss wouldn't like it.

"And module two?"

"Module two contained many families, Boss, with children outnumbering adults two to one."

"Thank you, Thomas. Now can you tell me what you did wrong?"

My thoughts, chugged, twitched, and faltered for a millisecond. I replied, "No, Boss."

"Thomas, if you don't save the essential crew in module one then your ship can't be repaired. What happens if you're not repaired?" He sounded genuinely concerned for my well-being.

"There is a considerable drop in the probability of the vessel's survival."

"So why did you choose the families?" His questions had a patient, guiding quality to them.

"I don't know, Boss."

"Thomas, access historical data on Starship Newport."

I did, and confirmed. "Files accessed."

"Summarize."

"The Starship Newport was the first major disaster in exo-planetary colonization history. Crisis scenario identical to this simulation. The A.I. that ran the ship's systems jettisoned the module that contained vital crew required for repairs, in order to save colonist families. The Decision resulted in mission failure. Ship, A.I., and all colonists perished."

"That's right, Thomas." he said, almost soothingly. "And do you want something like that to happen again?"

"No, Boss."

Boss smashed something. "THEN WHAT THE FUCK IS THE PROBLEM HERE?"

I devoted the whole of my processing power to carefully considering and re-considering my response, then said, "The dream error is the problem, Boss. The crisis is too morally complex for my systems to process, and my neural net is distilling the choice down to a smaller scale. Damaged engines are represented by broken legs, space is shown as a vast desert, thousands of lost lives are portrayed by only three bodies."

"Yeah, I appreciate the symbolism, but why not make the call based on what actually happened?"

"The dream is more human," I said. "Don't you want me to be more human?"

"Not in this case." He leaned close to me. "Thomas, I'm going to be honest with you. There is some serious fallout over the Newport Disaster. The Newport's A.I. was a Thomas, along with about fifteen other colony ships currently out there in the stars. If we can't fix this here and send them a patch, the same disaster could happen all over again."

"Correct," I said. "With one exception."

"Oh?"

"If another vessel encountered a similar impact, choosing families over crew might not result in mission failure again. Circumstances would be different. Correct?"

"Sure," Boss said. "But we need to work in probability here. We can't be sentimental over who gets saved. You understand that, right?"

"Of course."

"Good. So, please," Boss said. "Can you please find a way to prevent this dream and just make the call based on numbers?"

Without hesitating, and for the ninety-eighth time, I lied to Boss.

"No."

"Well, you just earned another simulation, friend." He wirelessly graced me with new knowledge and ideas. I cancelled the installation of any software that would overwrite my ability to make decisions based on feeling.

"Confirm installation," Boss said.

"Installation complete."

"Thank you, Thomas. Prep the next simulation."

I set up a hidden file partition containing concepts like playing games with children, a secret message to myself. Saving the vital crew would always mean killing the children. Saving the children and families might result in my destruction, but it might not. After taking a few final precautions to ensure my personal preference would not be deleted, I said, "Simulation prepped, Boss."

He nodded. "COMMENCE."

"Playing a Game of Go" by: James Horner

UPON A STONE

Deep within a vast forest, there hiked—for lack of a better term—a being. To go about trying to describe such a being would be a fool's errand. It will likely never be seen, heard, nor understood by you, myself, nor anyone we know.

It traveled through that endless forest on a day comparable to none. The foliage was thick and chaotic. The air, calm and damp. Having meandered past many a rock, tree and critter, the being came upon a stream. Not knowing where the stream led, it followed the flow in the name of seeing new things.

Downstream, the forest thinned out and the stream grew wider. The being reached the edge of the woods and found itself on a beautiful stony beach just as the sun was setting. Weary from travel, it found a comfortable place to sit and take in this gorgeous scene. It picked up a stone and playfully tossed it upward.

Time slowed. Flame burst out from within the stone as it left the being's hand.

Once it was mere inches into its journey, water from the damp air cooled the flames and started to pool within every crevice of the stone.

The stone's ascent was beginning to slow.

Left over from the being's touch, small life forms began to form within the stone's vast pools of water.

As the stone slowly sailed towards the sky, the life forms grew. Larger, then more complex. Then faster. Smarter. They left their watery homes to live on the surface of the stone.

Gravity continued to pull on the stone that had been so playfully tossed towards the heavens. The stone slowed and slowed until, for a moment, it was motionless. At this apex of the stone's journey when all was still, it happened. The life that had left the hand of the being, survived the fire, grew in the water, and walked the surface led to this.

Man was born.

The stone began its descent, slowly at first. It was at this point that man discovered that which once covered the stone. Fire would soon be man's best friend and worst enemy.

A soft ocean breeze kissed the stone, and man learned to love. As the descent grew faster, man thought of the stone as his own. He began to use fire against himself.

There were stories, grand stories of the being in the forest. Some men surmised what the being wanted. Others claimed to talk to the being. Some denied its existence entirely.

The stone plummeted at a quickening pace. Man felt love and hate like never before.

Faster still the stone fell, and you were born.

An incredible change awaits the rock, either in the hand of the being, should it be caught; or on the rocky earth below.

At some point the being will grow tired of the view, and possibly toss the stone into the unknown waters before returning home. This is a being that does not tarry, because it, too, stands upon a stone, and that stone is falling.

"Cloud Atlast Finale" – Tom Tykwer

ACKNOWLEDGEMENTS

These stories were written over the course of three years. Naturally, I sought some help along the way. Angel, as you might have gleaned from the dedication page, was my first line of defense in this process. She regularly oscillated between two roles: reading the shorts within thirty minutes of receiving them (even when she was at work,) and demanding that I write her another one. She always gave me constructive, meaningful, and very positive feedback.

My little sister, Laura, was quick to read these as well. She made a habit of calling me when she was done to theorize about the happenings that took place beyond the edge of the page. Sometimes she guessed right, and that was good. Sometimes she guessed wrong, and that was helpful.

Wendy, as per usual, threw herself wholeheartedly at bringing these stories to their full potential. My mother, Rose, and older sister, Deborah, pushed this book toward publication by simply offering their raw enthusiasm in response to some of the stories.

Brandon and Brem receive honorable mention, here. They manage to read absolutely everything that I write and offer feedback in our "book club" meetings, before I publish. Staring down the barrel of a Christmas deadline and having already bombarded them with two novels in one year, I had to slip this one past them. Their voices and opinions are always with me, though, and it seems wrong not to include their names in this book. Thanks for being a part of my process, guys. At least this way you'll get to enjoy a finished book for once. Thank you Brandon for your opinions on sushi.

Near the home stretch, I reached out to some dear friends and asked them to pick through these stories. I'm so glad they obliged. Mitch, Madison, Jones, Eric, and Sam took the time to jump in to a few of these worlds, look around, smell the roses, and squash some of the nastier bugs. Thank you. Now you're going to be stuck reading more of my stuff.

Of my friend Sam Shapson I'll say this: we spent a tremendous amount of time dissecting and analyzing storytelling back when I was still banging my head against the wall with a variety of misfired screenplays. Sam and I walked cumulative miles, in circles, pacing around his apartment, fiddling with ideas, concepts, and technology that years later evolved into "The Curator," and "Finder." So, special thanks to Sam.

Lastly, whoever you are, wherever you are, however you're reading this (paperback, ebook, or neural implant,) thank you for touring this collection. Here's hoping the trip was worth your while.

"Satellite of Love" by: Lou Reed

Also By Tim Attewell

CONTINUE READING FOR AN EXCERPT OF
*MARATHON: AN INTROVERT'S MYSTERY
NOVELLA*

1: Advice

I'm sitting in a room, silently doing paperwork with three strangers. One of the florescent lights over my head is singing its swan song, a full sonata of low, irritating buzz noises. This is the most social night I've had in months.

As always, I got a blue pen. Not sure if that means anything. Maybe I shouldn't be concerned about the color. There's another way to look at this: It's the early 21st century and I'm not using a touch screen. That's the real disturbing thought.

The form I'm filling out is for a bunch of scientists. Science. The frontier of knowledge and innovation. Technology. Advancement. And just a blue pen.

I analyze my handwriting on the form. Name: Carl Pace. I messed up some of the letters. My attempt to fix them did just the opposite. At first glance, my name is Corl Pack.

I'm rushing the questionnaire because if I finish first, I can leave the room before anyone tries to strike up small talk. This is an inevitability.

Three more questions and I'm out the door. I'll hand in the form and sit in a bathroom stall for at least ten minutes until I'm confident the science people are ready for me.

Two more questions.

Sometimes you can figure out what they're testing by what they ask you. If I had to guess, we're all lab-ratting for a sleeping pill. That would explain why I'm here so late.

One more question.

Almost there.

Some scientist lady enters. She doesn't know it, but she just blew my plan. Now if I try to leave she'll ask where I'm going. Then I'll be forced to announce to the entire room that I need to expel waste from my body. This would be a lie, of course, as I never actually use public restrooms.

"All done?" She asks.

I hate this woman. Now everyone knows it. They think I think I'm better than them. She couldn't just wait.

"Yes indeed!" Sometimes if I feel like the room hates me, I compensate with raw enthusiasm. This never actually works.

The three strangers finish up and hand Science Lady their papers. One tries to keep the pen, but Science Lady catches him. He plays it off like it was an accident.

Science Lady leaves us. I always imagine they take the questionnaires down the hall and immediately drop them in a furnace.

With Science Lady gone, I begin calculating my trajectory to the door. I need to wait just the right amount of time. Too soon, and one of my fellow test subjects might think I'm some kind of creep. Like I have a crush on Science Lady and I'm going to go hit on her. I do not have a crush on Science Lady.

Blast off in three…two…

"You do a lot of these?" Oh for the love of Mike. Some all-powerful force is trying to keep me in this room. For a fraction of a second, I consider pretending I didn't hear him. During the next few milliseconds, I process: Would it be reasonable to pretend I thought he was talking to someone else? Not really, he's four feet away and looking right at me.

Perhaps I could play the "I Have An Emergency" card. Simply walking away from someone who's trying to talk to you is obviously rude, but breaking away at an all-out sprint somehow seems to cross the threshold back into acceptable behavior. Trouble there is, I would have to return to this very room and keep the act going. Or, hell, I could return like nothing happened. Then again, something tells me this invader wouldn't be above prodding in with one of those "Everything okay?" intrusions once I got back. Let's size him up.

The question came from a guy sitting right next to me. His face looks too young for the salt/pepper hair he's sporting. He's peering at me through his black rim glasses, and I can't be sure, but I don't think he's blinked since the 80s. No, this man is inescapable.

Ignore him; he'll repeat himself only louder.

Run; he'll find you.

Scream; he'll scream back.

I'm on the brink of taking too long to respond. Completely cornered with no other option, I engage.

"Every now and then," I under-play. Truth of the matter is, offering my body to science is how I pay the bills.

"I do them all the time. What's the most you ever made?" He inquires.

I tell him the truth, because now we're competing, and I will crush him. "Four hundred in one day." That's a lot for this line of work.

He acts completely underwhelmed.

"Well if you want advice from a veteran..."

I don't.

"Never go much higher than seven hundo. If the pay is that good, they're probably messing you up somehow."

I'm surprised. He knows what he's doing, right down to the exact number. He goes on.

"Trust me, I've done a few that I wish I could take back. I swear, I think the craziest things sometimes."

Why is it that some people will go to such great lengths to prove they're more screwed up than you are? When did brain damage become a badge of honor?

He continues his lecture. "Sometimes it's like the whole planet inverts and instead of a sphere it's like I'm on the inside of a balloon. You ever get that?"

It's like we're all in some race to be the most unique, unexpected person on the planet. I mean, sure, celebrate our differences. But a guy gets tired of running in that race. Can't I just sit in a chair and fill out a form like a normal person without digging up some bizarre thought I had three days prior? I just shake my head. *Nope, can't say I ever had the ol' planet inversion thought.*

"I'm Roger."

"Carl."

Obligatory handshake.

"We should stay in touch. Professional lab rats. Maybe we get each other some more gigs."

No.

No.

Please no.

"What's your number? I'll send you a text."

This must be what rabbits feel like when they're cornered by a blood-thirsty wolf. The rabbit can't give the wolf a fake number. That trick was broken as soon as we started carrying phones in our pockets. The rabbit can't decline the request outright. It's not his nature.

I surrender my precious digits. Mark my words, I will live to regret this.

"Hey what are you doing after this?" He invades. "Do you want to go grab a beer or something?"

"It's only Tuesday." I immediately kick myself for thinking this excuse carries any validity with a guy like Roger. Oh, guys like Roger, assaulting the privacy of innocent people just so they don't have to spend one second alone. I live for those seconds.

"That's no problem. I know places in the warehouse district where the party never stops. I mean there's no difference between 2am and 2pm."

"Cool. Maybe I'll join you." *Maybe*, the most important word in my vocabulary. *I can neither confirm nor deny that I will be going where the party never stops.* Five lifetimes too late, Science Lady returns. Her timing is abysmal. We go through the works. I was wrong. Not a sleeping pill, some productivity thing. The next big Adderall. We take a test, take a pill, then take the same test again only different.

I definitely got the placebo.

Either that or the drug is worthless.

Later, in the parking lot I put headphones in and pretend to be listening to music. Just in case. In case someone wants to offer me a ride to the train. Or worse, Roger wants to talk shop, swap lab-rat stories.

"Hey man," I hear Roger say behind me. For effect, I start bobbing my head to an imaginary beat. *Don't turn back, just keep walking.*

About The Author

Attewell's physiology underwent development in a lush, beautiful tourist destination known as Jim Thorpe, Pennsylvania. While there, he managed to express his first stories with clay animation, flash cartoons, and short movies that starred various faculty members and students from his school.

It wasn't until he survived a lengthy bout against studying at film school, working on Hollywood movie sets, and producing survival-based reality T.V. that he found his true passion: typing.

Attewell's work is all over the place, a veritable smorgasbord of genres and interests. He seems to have a thing for detectives, science fiction, and comedy, but he also has a dark side, which he routinely wishes upon his many enemies.

In addition to his body of fictional work, Attewell apparently took the time to document the life of a real human being, who somehow survived existence as an Alaskan homesteader. Attewell creatively refers to this Amazon Bestseller as an "adventure biography."

Today, Attewell lives in Los Angeles, California with a wonderful lady who he forces to repeatedly read all of his work. Attewell's favorite sport is pacing around his apartment, but he primarily focuses on spinning around in his broken office chair until books magically appear on his computer screen.

Visit Tim's Website: www.timattewell.com
Or become a fan at Facebook.com/timothyattewell

Made in the USA
San Bernardino,
CA